REDEEMING VIKTOR

ALEXIS ABBOTT

PATHFORGERS PUBLISHING

Want to keep up to date with all my new releases, sales, and giveaways? What about getting a **Free** bad boy romance novel? Subscribe to my VIP Reader List:

http://alexisabbott.com/newsletter

I'm a stripper. It's a job. It's not who I am.

And like any job, we're here to work, make the most money we can, and go home to live our lives. We wear skimpy clothes, we dance to titillate and excite the customers, but none of us are in here with the first thoughts in our mind being anything but: let's make some cash and get home.

And I like my job. I'm good at it. I get to dress in sexy outfits, I work hard, and I come home at the end of the night exhausted and able to pay all my bills.

Sure, every now and then, I get to see handsome men. Even dance for them. And dancing for a handsome man is nice, of course. It's fun to dance for a handsome man over a grungy, smelly one. But all the girls in here would much rather dance for a *generous* man than a handsome one.

I'm not here to meet guys, after all. If I wanted that, I'd just head to a regular bar, soak up free drinks and compliments, and let the guys try to sweep me off my feet. Instead, I have to hustle and convince as many people as possible that having me dance for them is worth $20 for three and a half minutes of non-happy-ending pleasure.

I'm not looking for love in this place.

But even I can admit that the guy I spot in the audience is a hunk.

He has that natural boyish charm, but sanded and chiseled just enough to make him rugged. He's broad in the shoulder, and he wears a nice, stylish shirt with the cuffs rolled up a bit. Though I can tell he probably bought it before he buffed up, because it clings to his bulging biceps and pecs, outlining just how beefy he really is.

That's my first clue of who this mystery hottie might be.

From my vantage point on the stage, perched in my 6" heels, I watch him as he grabs a drink.

I love being on stage. Not only does it allow me a chance to scope the room, but it gives me a thrill to know how many men are watching me in my skimpy bikini. Wanting to give me money for my time.

I'm in the zone up here, and my chosen music thrums through me. I move to the rhythm of the song, letting all the room's good energy flood into me, but all the while my eyes are on him. I smile at him coyly as he turns to face me, and I lick my lower lip tantalizingly.

Whenever I flip my blonde hair, or touch my tanned skin, it's titillating, to me and the crowd.

I guess that's why I'm so good at my job. I treat it like a business, like an investment in my future, and I take it seriously, but I still have a hell of a lot of fun. I meet interesting people, I buy as many cute outfits as my budget allows, and yea, I'm a bit of an exhibitionist. I love being watched. To feel like I'm being a little bit bad, and there's a thrill of never knowing who I might meet.

The mystery hunk leaves the bar and comes to the stage, shirking the other dancers that approach him for private dances.

His eyes belong to me.

That's a powerful feeling, I'll admit. When I've got a man in my tractor beam, pulling him in as I dance upon the stage. I love knowing how entranced he is by me showing everything I've got under the dark lights. I have nowhere to hide. But why would I want to?

Most guys are cheap, and that goes doubly so for guys who come up to 'pervert's row', the lineup of seating along the stage. After paying for cover and drinks, a lot of them just want to sit back and look. But this guy, with his broad jaw, his handsome smile, and crew cut hair holds out a twenty.

Make that the second clue as to who he really is.

I don't often see twenties up on stage. A good tip is typically a five, maybe a ten if I'm lucky. After all, it's the cost of a private dance, just for watching me do what I was going to do anyways on stage. A twenty means he really wants my attention, and I'm only too happy to oblige him.

I lick my lips as I kick my legs out, swinging around the pole before gracefully landing on my knees, right in front of him. My legs are spread, and though I'm still in my holographic bikini, it doesn't leave much to the imagination. My heart is pounding to the rhythm of the music as I grin at him seductively.

"Baby," I breathe out as my hand reaches for his jawline, caressing it smoothly. "Is this your way of asking me on a date upstairs?" I ask, motioning to the VIP lounge.

"Oh yeah," he says in a deep, husky voice that speaks of raw masculinity. It's the kind of voice you imagine has no trouble getting the attention of a room when raised: raw, hard, and a bit gravelly. And that moment up close as I stroke his jawline, I see the tell-tale little scars. They're not disfiguring, in fact on a guy like him, they only add to his rugged appeal.

But that's the third and final clue I need as he watches me, entranced by my show. This guy's definitely a vet. We get our fair share in Vegas. After all, the city was originally developed to be an entertainment centre for men coming and going to the wars overseas. Our troops needed entertainment and relaxation, and a place to spend their cheques, and modern Vegas was the place to be.

I've danced for military guys before, lots of them. Most of them come in with uniform on; they love the extra attention it gets them. But the sexy man at the stage tries to hide it. He tries to blend in and look like a regular, handsome dude in a nice, stylish shirt. But I can tell. I've learned to watch people in here.

"Hope that's enough to break the ice," he says, his chin with an attractive cleft, his cheeks dimpled just a bit as he smiles at me.

I smile, biting on the corner of my lip seductively as my fingers go between my breasts. I grab at the string that holds my bikini together as I lean in towards him, whispering in his ear.

"What do you think?" I ask, just before I pull back and tug on my bikini string, letting the elastic fiber bounce away from my breasts, exposing myself — and my hard little nipples — to a man I don't even know. It's enough to send a shiver of excitement down my spine.

He's captivated, and though he's not the only guy at the edge of the stage tipping, he's the one tipping far more than any other. That makes him worth my time business-wise, even if I'm frankly just enjoying looking at this tall man's handsome face. He's the kind of guy I'd definitely want to hit on me in a regular bar, so I might be feeling a little generous too.

"I think you're the most beautiful woman I've ever laid eyes on," he husks out in a deep voice that's all conviction and truth. He's not bullshitting me. Not that he has any reason to, dishing out twenty buck stage tips. He's got that VIP dance on lockdown already.

No, it's the way he says it, the way his emerald eyes sparkle as he eyes my every movement and appreciates my body. This man is smitten. "I'd follow you to hell and back. So bring on the VIP section," he declares with a wry, uneven smile that only makes him all the more appealing.

I gotta admit, my stone-cold business attitude is fading the more I look at him. The more I listen to him.

It's not just the tips.

He's so hot that I'd be too shy to approach him outside of the club. In here, it's my sanctuary. I am my persona. I am Aphrodite, blonde bombshell with the extensions and fake lashes and an easy smile.

Outside these walls, I'm a much more simple Alice, who spends her time mostly with her Kindle and her rescue cat that has six toes.

My stage name, my elaborate outfits and makeup, they're like my superhero mask I pull on, and once I pull them off, no one knows who I am. I prefer it this way, most of the time.

Until I see a gorgeous guy and wish I'd met him outside the club, because holy hell I would love to wake up next to him.

I nuzzle his cheek and give him another smile. "You got it, baby. Just let me finish this song, and I am all yours," I say sweetly, dragging on the words.

"I'll do my best to sit politely by and wait. But no promises," he says with a bright grin and a wink. He's a charmer. Big, bulky, all muscle, his shirt red but the cuffs and collar a lovely accented piece that's got curious patterns. Most guys in Vegas look like uncaring tourists or guys who don't feel compelled to compete with uncaring tourists.

Though honestly, he could be in a sweat suit and I'd still be into him. Somehow, I know he'd still rock the look.

I walk towards the pole again and grab it in my hand, pulling myself up as I begin to spin. As I said, I like to feel like a superhero, and performing elaborate pole tricks is one of my powers. I always feel rejuvenated and powerful as I contort my body, letting people stare at my long legs and ample curves.

I keep it slow and sensual as the sounds of whistling fill the air. More cash fills the stage, and my mystery hunk is captivated as I invert my body, holding myself in the air before letting myself plummet back to the stage gracefully. I stop my descent just inches before my head would've hit the ground, and I strike a pose to much applause.

It's such a rush, and knowing I already have a dance lined up helps motivate me to give a better stage show. I always feel more confident knowing I'm not going to have to be approaching a dozen guys hoping one will say yes to my offer.

With my mystery man throwing out generous tips, it gets the other guys going as well. They're competing with him for my attention, and it's delicious. The one thing that turns me on in this place is money.

Well... the one thing that turned me on before he walked in. I fuck him with my eyes, letting them go heavy and lidded as I seductively lick my lips. I'm turning myself on with my fingers, touching over my soft skin, thinking about how much I couldn't wait to feel *his* hands on me. I pretend they're his, and my nipples stiffen until they almost ache.

I picture his tongue running along my nipple, tugging it into his mouth and suckling on it. I can't help but moan as my fingers go between my thighs, and graze along my bikini bottoms. My clit throbs with the sensation, and I bite my lower lip to suppress another sigh of pleasure.

And all the while, I stare at him with desire. I don't have to fake my arousal, not this time. I've never felt this way before. I've danced for hot guys before, but they tend to be cheap. They just come to strip clubs for the novelty, and don't like paying for something they think they can get for free.

But a hot man paying big money for me to dance for him? That's enough to make my knees quiver and my body to tense with desire and anticipation.

The song finally winds down, breaking me from my stupor, and the DJ announces, "That was the beautiful Aphrodite! Don't forget, you can get $20 dances on the floor, or take one of these luscious ladies up to the VIP for some real fun for just a little bit more!"

I grab my top and the bills around the stage, stuffing them in my purse before going to the only man that matters in my life right now: Military stud. It was the most lucrative stage show I've had in weeks, and by the time I reach him, I'm practically giddy with excitement.

He even offers me his arm like a gentleman, that thick forearm of his bulging with muscle and protruding veins, more than happy to escort me on up the stairs to the VIP room.

"I can't believe there's women like you in the world, in or out of the club," he says to me with that deep, appreciative voice of his. He has a way with making me feel like the only woman in the world that matters. "You must work at it 24/7 or been blessed by God above to look half as good as you do."

I laugh, trying to play cool, but already a flush is rising to my cheeks. Oh, he's a charmer alright. And maybe it's just the fact that he's so damned hot that his compliments are getting to me like they are. It's not like I haven't heard every line in the book, but usually it's from someone that is either twice my age, or just not my type.

"Hi Tom. This gentleman and I are going back for..." I say to the VIP host before looking at Military stud, waiting for him to answer.

"Until my wallet runs dry, if I'm being honest with my estimate," the stud says, forking over several bills. "Put me down for at least a half hour, huh?" he remarks, flashing me a look from the corner of my eyes.

"I'm not one for strip clubs, but... now I wish I'd stumbled in here sooner, just to meet you."

"Well it's my lucky night," I say, and yes, I'm being honest. Making money is why I'm here, but enjoying making money? That makes me very, very lucky.

I pull open the purple curtain, revealing the rounded bench with velvety fabric and a small drink table in the middle. I close it behind us, and a new song comes on, some softer rock music than the techno and heavier stuff downstairs. I like the VIP room. It's private, comfortable, and pays my rent.

"When was the last time you were in a club?" I ask as we both settle in.

"It's been four years," he says without missing a

beat, and if I needed another clue, that was it. That's the maximum tour length for military guys, and I guess that makes me his first stop back. "Been away working, needed a reminder of what it's like to look at beautiful women. Wasn't counting on an overdose though, so be prepared to call for assistance carting me out," he jokes.

"Don't worry, I'll take good care of you," I say as I straddle his lap.

But for a second, I forget where I am. It's almost like a skip in time, and I'm staring at this gorgeous man, feeling his body against mine, wrapping my arms around his neck, and it all just feels right.

Like it's fate. Like it's meant to be.

I know it sounds cheesy. I'm not really one to believe in signs, or at least, I never did until now.

I shake my head to try to chase away the strange shock, but I'm still staring at the most handsome man I've ever seen, and I gotta be honest.

It feels a little like love.

I know it's not. I don't even know him, but if love at first sight exists, this has to be what it feels like.

"I never got your name," I say softly, still stunned by the weird experience. I must be losing my touch. Or maybe my mind. The VIP section is supposed to be for the client's fantasies, not my own. But what harm is there in indulging in my own lurid fantasies about what I want to do with him?

"Viktor," he says. He doesn't mind in the least

that I'm not really dancing for him. His two big, rough hands rest on my hips, not groping where he shouldn't but squeezing me ever so slightly. "My dad was a Ukrainian immigrant, that's where the name comes from. Just so you know I'm not the creator of Frankenstein," he says, his nostrils flaring, taking in my scent as he stares. Soaks me in.

That makes me genuinely, earnestly laugh. I never expected him to have a bit of literary humor in him, and I have to cover my mouth as my eyes still sparkle at him.

Why couldn't I have met him out of the club? Things could be so delicious.

"That's terrible. But I'm Aphrodite. And I really am the Goddess of lust and romance."

"Knew it without you saying a thing, and don't doubt it for a second," he says without missing a beat, and again, I know he means it. Not the least of which because I can feel the real results of his desire beneath me as I sit in his lap. A hefty bulge right there in my perch. "From the moment I walked in the door, I knew I was in the presence of divinity. If I was a smarter man maybe I would've hightailed it out before you could turn me into your newest and greatest worshipper."

"Greatest, mmm?" I purr in his ear as I begin to lightly grind in his lap, my hand stroking through his wheat-blonde hair. "And what will make you my absolute greatest worshipper, Viktor?"

I get a low groan from him, a satisfied husky sound that's delightful on the ear. But the way I bring this mighty, mountain of muscle to a quiver is the best part. He wants me so bad, and I want him too.

"I don't wanna say and spoil the moment," he says, his voice deeper, more gravely as he wraps those arms around me and holds me tight, letting his palms rest just at the edge of my ass below.

My skin prickles with desire, and I twitch my ass muscles a little, grinding against him as I do so.

"You can touch lower," I whisper, biting my own lip to hide my excitement.

I'm already soaking my little bikini bottoms, and I'm almost nervous he's going to notice soon. I've never felt like this, dancing for a client. It's like the rest of the world has simply fallen away, leaving us in its wake.

He's a gentleman, doesn't touch where he's not supposed to, but he's no fool. And the moment I give him go ahead, those big strong hands sink down, cupping my ass cheeks, sinking his powerful fingers into them as he gives a delighted, rough groan.

"I don't wanna be that sucker client that over-steps his bounds and makes shit weird. I don't wanna say anything that'll send you running," he tells me, letting his eyes nearly shut as he looks me over, enjoys the sensation of our bodies together while the music plays. "I'd love to ask you on a date, but instead I'll just say I hope this night never ends."

My heart is beating faster in my chest, and I'm trying to remain professional, but I can hardly believe this hottie wants to go out with me. I know the stereotype is that strippers are all full of themselves, but most of us are as self-conscious as other women, we just hide it better.

"You're hoping time stands still?" I ask seductively, but my mind is going back to when I first touched him and how it felt as though time did exactly that.

"Up here with you? Absolutely."

I let out a soft moan, and I grind into him again before I feel a shiver go through me, and I know if I keep going, I'm going to come in his lap.

I've never came in a client's lap.

But those big strong hands of his knead my ass cheeks, those thick, muscular forearms bulge and squeeze in against me on either side, egging me on, grinding me atop his lap and that impressive bulge. He's turning me into everything I'm not. Everything I never thought I could be.

Those handsome looks, that natural charm, the rugged experience from a hard life serving, it all makes him hard to resist. And then, to top it all off, he leans in and murmurs in my ear. That rough, low voice of his like a verbal vibrator, stimulating my brain to climax.

"If I met you anywhere else, I'd make it my life's mission to win you over and make you my girl," he says, wetting his lips slowly as he gives a low moan from the lap dance. "I'm just glad I never met you four years ago, or I'd have gone AWOL to chase you like a dog in heat."

A jolt of electricity goes through me, and even though I want to hold back and suppress this exquisite pleasure from going through me, there's nothing I can do to stop it. I can't hold back the tide of pleasure any longer.

I'm grinding him more aggressively as I come in his lap, my breathing peppered with moans against his ear as I ride out the explosive high.

It's an overwhelming sensation, and I know he's noticed. Those big, muscular arms keeping me rocking even after my mind has long since lost control of my body. His chiseled jaw, just lightly stubbled, brushing my cheek as he helps guide me through the earth-shattering climax.

"Fuck you look even more gorgeous when you come," he breathes into my ear, his first time crossing that boundary from client to something more. And he didn't do it unprovoked. Nobody could accuse him of being inappropriate. It was me who had lost my cool and did something I shouldn't have.

"Oh my god," I whisper, embarrassment suddenly taking over me. This is so unprofessional. How did I get so carried away? But I pull back and look at him, and I'm smitten all over again. I can't bear to look at him and I duck my face away. "Oh god, I'm so... I shouldn't have... I didn't mean to..."

"It's okay," he assures me, his grip relaxing, no longer holding me into that tight, delightfully carnal embrace. "Don't worry. I don't presume nothin'. Trust me, it was a show worth more than what I have in my bank account," he says with a charming smile. "Besides, if I'm being honest, I'm just relieved it wasn't me who popped his load from this. You've got me on edge, babe."

"I've never, ever..." I swear, but I can't actually bring myself to say it. He's completely torn down my walls, my Aphrodite personae slipped away. I'm just simple Alice in his lap, even with the fake 'lashes and six-inch stilettos. I'm naked often in the club and with clients, but he's the first one that ever made me feel exposed.

I bite in on my lower lip, gnawing it for a second as I stare at him.

"It's alright," he says in that thick, assuring voice of his. And though he's still rock solid hard beneath me, he just gently caresses my sides. He has self-control in spades. "Fuck, trust me, it did nothing but assure your place as the Goddess of romance and lust in my mind," he says with that disarming charm of his again.

"Did you mean what you said about wanting to ask me out?"

I've managed to stun the handsome Viktor, making him hesitate a moment. And though I worry, he wipes that all away fast.

"I would fight every man in this club for the simple shot at asking you out," he says, his deep emerald eyes sparkling as he gazes at me, so full of desire and a tenderness not common to big, muscular brutes like him. "Will you go out with me?" he asks.

We've been back here for so long that the VIP host pulls aside the curtain before I can answer. "You guys still going?"

It's been a half hour, and I haven't moved from his lap. I'm still wearing my bikini, and I just had one of the most intense orgasms of my life.

"Ah, I think Viktor has to go. We're just finishing up, Tom. Thanks for checking," I say.

"Ah shit," Viktor says, reaching for his wallet in his pants pocket. "Lost track of time with you. Feels like it's only been a minute," he says, pulling out a fat wad of twenties. "What do I owe you? Fuck it, this is probably enough, right?" he says, forking over way more than enough to cover it.

I nod and hand Tom his tip, and he leaves us alone once more.

"It's late enough that I can leave now. If you're ready for that date."

He looks taken aback. He must've been thinking I was dismissing him, because his stunned look slowly transforms to one of pure excitement.

"Fuck yeah, I am," he says. He stands, lifting me as effortlessly as when I grab my purse. Well… more accurately, he lifts me as effortlessly as I lift the coin purse inside it. "I can take you to a nice restaurant, well… might be too late for a lot of those, but we could find something."

"It's Vegas, honey. There's always something open," I say with a small roll of my eyes. "Or we could head back to my hotel for room service. It's nothing flashy," I warn him.

What am I saying? What am I doing? Inviting him back to my room! The Alice part of me recoils in horror.

"I'll do ya one better," he says with a playful boastfulness. "You can come to my hotel. I splurged for one fancy ass room; you'll love it," he says, squeezing my thighs as he holds me up in his arms. "Figured I'd make the most of my time in the city. Suddenly glad I did."

"How can I say no to that?"

Anyone would say I was crazy to go home with a stranger from the club. If I turned up dead in the morning, a bunch of people would cluck their tongues at reading the story of how I died, and what I did, and say, "serves her right". That's one of the biggest drags about my job. A man could kill me and it'd be 'my fault'.

But this spark between us is real. It's not something I can walk away from. The entire time I've spent with him, I've felt like it's been something special happening, and I could desperately use something special right now. I'm not a big believer in signs or fate, but him walking into my life... It feels like there is something larger than life at work, and I'd be a fool to ignore that.

The entire ride to the hotel is spent with excitement thrilling up and down my veins. It feels like it takes so long to get there, even though it's only a half hour trip. But as we pass the glittering Vegas attractions, I gaze at him with such fascination. He is, without a doubt, the hottest guy I've ever laid eyes on. Every so often, he catches my gaze and smiles at me. His hand clasps mine, and it feels almost chaste after our explicit time in the champagne room.

But even that sweet touch makes my heart pound, the energy between us undeniable.

He's staying at one of the newer hotels right near the strip, a very swanky three-tower complex that shimmered gold in the Vegas sun during the day.

At night, they stand like pillars of wealth and good -- if slightly ostentatious -- taste.

He stops at the front desk on the way up to order a bottle of wine and a fancy meal, but the entire time, I'm hanging off him like a groupie. He feels so good against my hands as I blatantly explore his chest, his arms, his palms... He's rugged, and has such a beautiful expression of desire on his face as he turns from the front desk towards the elevator.

We're giggling like kids as we race each other to hit the button, but before the elevator can even ding, he has me pressed against the wall, his mouth meeting mine with such hunger. My tongue dances with his as I soften into his aggressive kiss, and when the doors open, we nearly stumble in like two love-drunk teens.

His fingers roam up my side, under my top, and I

blush, because I know every single public inch of Vegas has a security camera attached to it. But I can't stop him. My entire body is filled with such a beautiful, powerful energy because of him, and I can easily see myself getting addicted to the sensation of his body on mine.

His mouth finds my throat, kissing it with a hard, bruising motion and I smile, knowing that tomorrow, I'll see the mark he left on me. I moan as my fingers go through his short hair, and his cock presses into my hips. My breathing is heavy as the elevator doors finally open on the top floor. He picks me up, my legs wrapped around his waist as he quickly carries me to his room.

He puts me down and stares at me with such intensity I have to avert my eyes for a moment. My blood is running hot, and all I want to do is fling myself onto his bed, but that's so not like me. Neither is making out with a stranger I met at the strip club, and nearly pouncing on him in the elevator. Viktor brings something different out in me, and I'm not sure how I feel about it.

I'm just about to wrap my arms around him when I hear a knock at the door. He frowns, obviously regretting ordering room service as I wander further into the suite, taking a look around.

He wasn't kidding when he said he splurged, because it's about ten times more room than a single man would ever need. It has it all: from a gorgeous balcony view overlooking the city and desert, to two bathrooms, and a spacious ensuite that is bigger than my whole hotel room put together.

When I make my way back to the living room, he's popping the cork on the wine.

"This is more money than I've spent on myself in probably five years, at least," he says with a chuckle, pouring us up two glasses of champagne.

"Well you earned it, you might as well spend it, right?"

Now that we're in his room, and the tension between us is broken, I don't really know how to act. I'm not the one-night-stand type of girl. I'm not even a sex on the first date kind of girl. And the lights feel so bright now, away from the muted darkness of the strip club. It suddenly all felt so... real. Like I'm really going through with it now.

As though he senses my discomfort with the bright lights, he dims them and gives me a seductive smile.

"Is that better?" he practically growls.

I nod, drawing in my lower lip as I stand in front of him with my skinny jeans, tank top and 6" heels.

"Much more what I'm used to," I grin as I take the glass of champagne, and we clink our glasses together.

"To finding that spark in surprising places," he says with a knowing smile.

His hand finds my hip, tugging me to him, and I

can still feel his cock throbbing beneath his pants. It feels like being such a bad girl, something that the Alice part of me is definitely not used to, despite my job.

He drinks down the glass of champagne in little time before topping us both off.

"I've never done this before, you know," I say nervously as I sip the second glass, letting its bubbles soothe me. I have to admit... I'm out of my league. I don't know what people are supposed to do on one-night-stands. Am I supposed to just start kissing him? Or is he supposed to kiss me? It's 2012, and I'm all about female empowerment, but I still have no idea what's normal.

Though he's been overseas for 4 years. He might not know either.

And that thing in the elevator... that was hot. It was spontaneous and exciting and it turned me on more than I could ever admit. So why am I feeling so self conscious now?

"And I've not done anything of this sort in a long, long time," he says to me. Completely belying his point, though, he reaches out and puts that big, strong arm of his around my waist and pulls me close to him. I can feel he's still rock solid in his nice looking pants, and that should be lewd and inappropriate right? But the way he looks into my eyes makes it feel anything but.

"You really are the most gorgeous woman I've

ever seen," he says before tilting his head and leaning in, placing a surprisingly soft, tender kiss upon my lips.

He tastes like peppermint, and my shoulders relax as soon as I taste him on me. All my worries suddenly disappear, and instead, there's just that spark. That feeling of rightness once more. I've never felt like this before. My stomach is filled with a thousand butterflies as his tongue presses against mine.

Earlier this evening, I was Aphrodite. Goddess of the strip club, queen of the stage. I was confident, in control of my world. But now I feel powerless, like I'm caught up in a current I can't fight. But I don't want to fight it. Especially not when those big, powerful, comforting arms of his put aside his champagne glass and hold me tightly. Those two big hands grasping my ass again as his kiss grows deeper, more intense. His tongue mingles with mine inside my mouth as we stand there in his posh room, making out like horny teenagers instead of the experienced adults we are.

I put my champagne glass on the bar, and both of my arms go around his neck. With my heels, I'm tall, but still nowhere as tall as he is, and my head cocks back as I feel a growl grow in his chest.

"You're so hot," I manage to say, breathily.

"Then we should make for one very, very hot couple together," he says with a wry grin on his face in the brief moment between our kisses. His big hands lift me back up, just as easily as he did in the club, carrying me into the air conditioned bedroom. It's a huge, spacious place, with a California-King-Size bed in the middle of the room.

But little things like that are lost quickly as he rests my back on the mattress, his big, brawny body atop mine as we make out. Our hips grind into one another like teens in the backseat of a car. Our passion is explosive, and we just want to touch and explore one another, and take things slow.

Well, as slow as we can, considering I just met him a few hours ago.

My jeans give me a little more protection than the micro bikini I wear in the club, but honestly, I'm still pretty close to coming already. He just has the magic touch. Everywhere his fingers trail on my body, I just comes alive. Every growl, every little nip of his teeth, every dance of his tongue does me in.

Is this what it feels like when you're someone's soulmate? Like he knows my body even though he's still a stranger?

He's been away for four years, but those hands of his are moving over me with an expert's touch. He's managed to undo my jeans without me even noticing it. Then his hands are pulling my tank top up over my head with a single motion that can only be described as smooth.

"Stunning," he says in the brief moment he has to

look me over before his hungry mouth goes to my neck, licking, nipping, and kissing at my skin.

He's already seen me almost completely naked, but back here, in his hotel, it's a whole different thing.

He never thought he'd be kissing my skin.

And I never thought I'd be grinding against his erection, desperate to feel him all over me.

Those hands of his — God, those hands! — They reach in behind me, undo the bikini top from my stage show, which I'm using in place of a bra. I'm topless again, and his mouth is moving down, devouring my chest, kissing around my pink areola and teasing it to a peak. His hands move onto my jeans again, tugging them down from my hips, eager to get me bare upon his large bed.

I squirm out of them, though it's hard, with his weight pinning me to the mattress. But by some miracle, they end up flung across the room, hitting the window which conveniently is a bit reflective. It means I get to see his body moving against mine, and I shudder with ecstasy at the perfect sight.

The view only gets all the better when he kisses and suckles upon my nipple. I watch my mouth as it parts into an o-shape, the pleasure so stark upon my expression. I can't remember ever seeing myself look so happy, so aroused, in all my life.

His sensual kisses and licks trail between the peaks and valley of my chest, exploring me and tasting my skin as my hands roam through his hair. I pull him to me, but he's strong and can easily resist me, instead taking what he wants.

Luckily, what he wants is just as delicious, and my moans are starting to pepper the air as I squirm beneath him. I can't ever remember being so turned on before, like my entire body is on fire. I just want him everywhere, it's driving me wild!

I can't tell if this is lust or something else. But all I know is that the usual Alice that I know would never be here without a good reason. She's cautious and thoughtful, and not at all impulsive.

There's a reason I'm here, pinned beneath him. Some greater design. Some type of fate. I'm meant to be here, having my nipples teased by this hotter-than-hades military man.

He flicks the hard little bud with his tongue before he reluctantly withdraws. Kneeling up on the bed, he unbuttons his shirt and shows me that he's everything I ever hoped he could be beneath.

It's all chiseled muscle under there. Bulging pecs, ripped abs, all peppered with some hair and a few little scars, some old, some fresh. But like the rest of him, it's just enough to give him that edge. That impression that this is a man who's seen and done things that few have.

His belt comes next, and he doesn't leave me waiting long before the pants follow. His boxer-briefs catch on his hip, and I can only see the very trunk of his cock. But it's thick, lodged just beneath a small tuft of blonde pubic hair.

He's an Adonis. Pure and simple. And that fits, because I'm his Aphrodite.

My hand reaches down for his cock, hungry to have it in my hand. I want to feel him throb against me and know that he wants me just as bad as I want him.

"Viktor," I mutter as I kiss his chest, my nose tracing a scar along his collarbone. He's so gorgeous, and I know he's dangerous, but he's been the perfect gentleman with me. Maybe that's part of the appeal. I know he could do things I'd never be able to dream of, lived through things I couldn't imagine, and yet with me, he shows such strength and willpower. He's not a brute.

He's everything a man ought to be.

My fingers — so slender next to the thick trunk of his massive manhood — grasp the edge of his underwear and tug them down. And down. And down. More and more of that length unveils so slowly until at last I pull them down far enough and that long, pulsating pillar leaps out against my arm, smacking my wrist with a meaty thud.

He has the biggest cock I've ever seen on a man.

"Oh babe," he mutters in a growly voice, and then reaches into his pants pocket, pulling out a condom and placing it down on the bed beside us as he runs his hand through my hair, relishing the feel of it.

"You came prepared," I tease, but I'm glad at least one of us is thinking clearly. I stroke him, my fake lashes fluttering down over my blue eyes as his cock throbs in my hand. He's so hot, his veins so pronounced, and he's had a near constant erection since we first met. I know he's busting for me, but he's making this moment last.

"Something they taught me," he says, his dick swelling in my hand. "Fuck, you're gonna make me pop if you keep that up. I haven't had a lady's touch in so long."

I know he's bluffing. He's made of sterner stuff than that.

His big, muscular body twitches as he tugs my bikini down, literally having to peel them from my slick slit. But my time holding onto his dick comes short as he moves down my body, parting my thighs and leaning in, taking a deep breath over my pussy.

"Ohhh fuck, you smell so good," he says, his nostrils flared in the brief moment before he lunges in and begins to devour me.

Four years without a woman? He's eating me out like a man who hasn't eaten food in nearly so long. His mouth wraps about my clit, sucking it for a moment before his tongue laps at my slit and on up to swirl about my sensitive little bud.

His fingers pry apart my thighs, resisting my attempts to clamp them down around his head, and the extra sensation drives me wild. I gasp, my body squirming as his tongue plays with me.

I'm already on edge, and my hands are gripping the comforter as I start to plead with him. I'm not even sure what I'm saying. It's all running together, breathy words that barely make sense, all peppered with *please* and *oh god*. I feel like I'm waking up for the first time in a very long time, actually able to feel everything with such an exquisite intensity.

He's a ravenous beast for me, the wet sounds of his mouth and tongue working my pussy filling the air. The only thing I can see is his broad, muscular shoulders hunched over, his emerald eyes sparkling as they occasionally look up from between my thighs to watch my breasts heave and my face contort with pleasure.

He's seen me come before, watched me orgasm on his lap. And he watches me now like there's nothing more in the world he wouldn't relish than seeing a rerun.

He doesn't have to wait long before my hand is on the back of his head and I'm screaming his name as I grind into his face. My spine arches in a feline manner and my head presses back into the pillow as another amazing jolt of electricity sparks through me.

Viktor doesn't let up though. He continues to tongue my gushing pussy through my climax, prodding and teasing my clit to such heights as he watches and relishes each moment. He keeps going stubbornly until my cries are dying down and I'm having to tug at the hair on the back of his head, unable to take any more.

He rises up then, his dick as hard as ever, jumping out from his groin as he licks at his lips, and wipes around his mouth, savoring my honey.

"Damn, I've never enjoyed eating a pussy as much as yours before," he growls out with lust before reaching for the condom, ripping it open and beginning the process of having to pull that tight sheath on over his impressive manhood. The glistening rubber clings to every contour of his rigid, veiny shaft to the point where I worry it might tear at any moment.

I'm still in a haze from... how many orgasms did he just give me? But I still appreciate the sight of the hulking, perfect man in front of me. As soon as he's suited up, I'm reaching out for his dick, basically begging for him.

I've never needed to be fucked as much as I need him right now.

He moans at my very touch, even separated by that thin sheath. But without hesitation, the two of us now well past the point of taking it slow, he lowers himself over me and gets between my thighs.

That gorgeous piece of equipment -- that the military most definitely did not gift him with -- lines up with my slit until he's pushing it down into me.

My pink little labia flowering around his shaft, stretching wide until I'm pushed taut around him as he sinks on in, balls deep.

"Are you okay?" he asks me, and at first I'm confused, but then I realize I've been crying out and moaning so loud he thought something was wrong.

"Better than okay," I say, and I try to laugh, but even that comes out as a moan. My legs wrap around his ass, and he's almost too big to handle, but I've never been wetter in my entire life, and that's definitely helping.

He kisses my lips and doesn't delay, those powerful hips of his beginning to pump into me, his deep, husky moans filling the air as we begin to screw atop his bed. It's the most intense love-making of my life, and as he builds speed it only gets better.

I can hear his heavy balls slapping against my butt noisily, his body angling itself just perfectly as he pierces into me deeper than any man ever had. He's a titan of sex, having not only the looks but the precise little ways of working my body down to perfection.

Or maybe it's just fate that we're both so perfectly made for each other.

Whatever it is, I can't believe it's so intense!

"Fuck!" he curses, and I can feel him tense and bulge inside me, his balls tightening, no longer slapping my ass so noisily. He's getting close.

"Come in me," I whisper, and I can't believe how

filthy the words sound off my tongue. What's gotten into me? But I like it, too. Whatever magic spark exists between us, it's turning me a little bit bad, and there's nothing more that I'd like than being bad with him.

He's stubborn though, and I can tell he's drawing it out just a bit longer as he reaches his thumb in, tweaking and torturing my poor little abused clit, sparking more pleasure through me as he pulses with desire, edging so close. So close… until…

"Coming!" he cries out, before giving such a deep, hoarse moan, burying himself into me balls deep as he climaxes. That thick shaft swells inside me as he loses all control and bucks into me, grinding his dick in deep as he empties those heavy balls.

And he's timed it perfectly with my... I've lost count. Another crashing orgasm. I've absolutely made a mess of his bed, and I still can't stop myself from grinding against him, letting that wave after wave crash over me until I'm utterly and completely spent underneath him.

We're panting together, his muscles all glistening with a thin sheen of perspiration, only adding more allure to his body. He's an Adonis alright. And I can't help but rub my hands all over those hard bulges, and appreciate every bit of him as he leans in and kisses me affectionately, none of his interest having waned.

We make out for a long while after, minutes

ticking away as we grind our bodies together, my pussy milking him for all he's worth, and when at last he pulls away, his dick still semi-hard inside me.

"You wanna go again?" he asks me with a devilish grin on his face.

"You're going to be the death of me," I say with a giggle, even as I nod my head eagerly.

He pulls back, and damn is it a beautiful view. His shoulders back, it only shows off his rippling physique all the better. Following the trail of hair on past his abs, down to his groin, and then…

We both see it at about the same time.

Instead of a little white bubble at the tip of the condom, we both stare at his dick, mostly raw and uncovered, except for a tattered band around his shaft.

The condom broke.

My first encounter with a woman in so long ended with a broken condom and a beautiful but panicked woman. It wasn't the picture perfect ending to my return from service, but fuck… nothing about it I'd take back.

I had reassured her, told her I'd help her with whatever comes, whatever she decides.

Then I asked her on a second date.

I mean, odds are likely nothing comes of it at all, right? People are careless all the time, so I tried to make sure she knew that.

But I won't lie, part of me is excited at the prospect. I'm ready to get back to normal life, or as close to one as I can get. I put all the years of service behind me, and all the ugly, nasty moments it entailed.

A new girl and, hell, even a baby, could only help

me get back to feeling like a normal man. What person wouldn't want that?

Both of us were feeling better before the night ended, and I held her 'til she fell asleep in my arms. I didn't get a wink myself. I didn't want to spoil that moment, and watching her slumber as the golden Vegas sun filtered in behind the curtains was one of the most serene moments of my life.

And when she woke up, I got that date.

Officially we're not supposed to meet until tomorrow night, but I wanted to come see her at work just before she gets off. Escort her back and let her know I'm thinkin' of her. Maybe all that time abroad, fighting endless battles has made me soft. Or maybe I always wanted to find the right woman, and now I feel like I have.

We're drawn to each other uncontrollably. She's the sexiest woman I've ever laid eyes on, and even though we only had that one night together, she couldn't sleep right after the broken condom.

I held her and reassured her for so long, but in the end we stayed up almost all night talking. About everything. I was able to really get to know her. Not just Aphrodite. I got to know Alice, and I'm even more smitten with her.

She told me about her plans for her life, and I told her about mine. I told her about how I was on my way for a new job with a military contractor in Vegas that paid well, and how someday I hoped to retire to the countryside where I was from. I wanted to start a business and return something to the community I was from. I hated to leave it as a kid, but there were no jobs, no prospects.

The marines were the only way out for me and my buddies. It was a way to serve my country and give something back. And it was also a way to get paid, get an education, and see the world beyond our little fishing town on the Maine coast.

But as with all young military men, we didn't all make it back. And of my small group that did, I'm even sadder to say that not all of my buddies made it back feeling up to life as a civilian again.

The best thing was... she was on my same wavelength. She, too, wants to get out of the city and find a simpler life eventually. I can't believe my luck that I found someone who so perfectly gets me. Someone who understands, and burns just as hot for me as I do for her.

I'm getting giddy as I near the club. I'm not gonna let the shit that happened overseas, the friends I lost to bombs, bullets or trauma drag me down tonight. I'm just going to focus on her. On us.

There's a beautiful girl I gotta win over.

It's that thought in mind when I pass by a small tussle. A big guy, round in the middle, is grabbing hold of a dancer on smoke break.

"Come on, you came with us last time," the big

guy says, pulling on her arm as she's tugging away with all her strength.

"Let go! I'll never go anywhere with the likes of you again!" she spits at him.

Then the big guy's friend — or more likely his bodyguard, judging by his attire and demeanor — steps in as she strikes out at the man. He restrains her, and as big and tall as he is, it's not hard for him to lock the svelte woman in place.

Instinct kicks in and I'm already in action. It's like a flip has been switched. As soon as I see that man lay a crude hand on the woman, I send a stiff elbow to his ribs before I say a word. That's probably the wrong approach for civilian life. I should've warned him first, but in the marines, I learned to respond before I think. That's how we out-survive our enemies.

"Let her go!" I bellow at him with another blow to his elbow that stuns his arm and makes him lose his grip. The dancer he was restraining kicks him in the groin and earns her freedom the rest of the way on her own.

"Assholes!" she says to the two guys, before shooting me a grateful look and heading inside.

The big guy is glaring daggers at me, but his bodyguard is cradling his arm and backing off. He knows better. He's learned his lesson... or the guy he works for simply isn't paying enough.

"Bah!" the big guy says, dismissively, calculating

that he's lost his only muscle. "Used that tart up anyhow." They turn to go to the parking lot as I stare them down, fists clenched. "Remember her pathetic sobbing by the end? 'No no! Stop! I didn't agree to this!'" the big guy says in a mocking tone.

My vision turns red.

I can see the woman again in my mind's eye, and her panic when she was grabbed. The way she said she'd never go with them again was the voice of a woman deeply traumatized. She was a tough woman, and she'd managed to sound angry and intimidating despite being in heels and a silk robe to shield her bikini clad body from unwanted view. But there had been a quivering to her voice. She'd been hurt. She was afraid.

She'd been raped.

He just said it. Laughed about it. Turned her pain into a joke.

Time stops meaning anything. The two of them are at the rich man's car, the bodyguard helping open the door for him when I set out. The big guy is inside, but before his helper can shut the door, I'm on him and slamming his head to the metal door, knocking him to the ground.

There's no thinking. There's no moralizing. There's no worrying. There's just acting. That's the way I was trained. That's who I am.

I yank that piece of shit out of his car and toss him against a concrete pillar at the edge of the lot. I hear him thud and cry out painfully, wind knocked from him. Before he can say a word though, I'm on him, pummeling him down.

I'm making him pay for what he did. I'm teaching him a lesson that he won't forget.

I was raised to believe that a real man uses his strength to protect those weaker than him. That a real man never takes the cowardly way out and uses his power in this world to prey on those beneath him.

That's what drove me to service. And that's what drives me to beat the shit out of this rich prick.

Even in my haze of rage, I know enough not to kill him. I can direct my blows to crack a few ribs, bust his nose and make him ache for a year, but I won't leave him dead. Just teach him a lesson.

"Don't you ever fuckin' touch another woman without her say so, you hear me?!" I bellow at him, yanking him by his collar before planting another punch in his gut.

That's it, I tell myself. I made the point. But I let myself get carried away; I underestimated the rich prick's guard. And a gun goes off at the back of my head.

Everything's dark.

Five years later...

When I first came to Vegas, it was to earn some big money to put away to save for my plans of running my own shop. A book-store and coffee shop, to be exact. That's what all my work had gone towards.

But a brief stopover in the glittering, neon city, became a long stay.

My first hope of romance didn't go so well. One night of passion ended there. A one-night-stand.

The money I make from dancing here is too good to pass up. Far too good when I've got a kid to worry about now too. Over four years old, my little Cierra is a blessing. I didn't get my store, and probably never will at this rate of trying to prepare for her future, but she's precious to me. I wouldn't trade her for the world.

A loud bang disturbs us as Cierra and I play in the living room.

"Where's that satchel of money I left on the counter?!" bellows John, my ex-boyfriend.

"You took it last night, said you had to deposit it, remember?" I call back. John's always got money laying around. He tells me he's a rich guy, but honestly, it goes faster than it comes. And if not for me, he'd never remember where it went.

"Shit, that's right," he said, running his fingers back through his hair.

He has his issues, but he doesn't mistreat Cierra, and he helps out with rent most of the time. She's my number one priority these days, so I haven't kicked him out since we broke up. But every time he has another outburst, I wonder if it isn't time for us to go our separate ways completely.

"Not in front of Cierra," I say with a sigh.

"Oh, yeah yeah," he says, looking more distracted than usual. He's a high-strung guy. And honestly I should've kicked him out when we broke up, months ago. In the beginning we split bills, but now it mostly falls to me, despite his claims of wealth. I put up with it, thinking it'd be temporary, but his issues have grown worse. He has a temper on top of everything else.

He's never hit me, but it's not the image of a man I want Cierra to grow up with.

I guess the only real blessing is I've never let her believe that John is her dad. I never wanted to lie to her, not about anything, and so I always insisted she called him John instead of Dad, much to John's annoyance.

I haven't told her who her dad was, not really. But when she was a baby, I'd tell her about how I'd fallen in love with Prince Charming. Love at first sight.

And that his name was Viktor.

But she doesn't know that's her dad. She's too young anyways, but I know eventually, those questions will come. Especially once she gets to school, she'll start asking questions fast about who her daddy is. I both dread and look forward to it, because as much as my heart aches with the memory, I love talking about Viktor.

About how he made me feel complete for just a few hours. About how being with him was the best thing I ever did, because it brought her into my life, and how the only regret I have is that I never saw him again.

That's one of the many reasons why John and I didn't work out, his violent temper aside. I was waiting for a guy who's stood me up for five long years. I guess he just got cold feet. Our first — and only — time together was intense, and I thought he was up for it, but I never heard from him again.

It's the type of heartbreak that few people know.

Love at first sight, never to see him again.

There's a lesson for her to learn there too: love can let you down. But I want her to know that my love — her mother's love — will never fail her, first. So that's why I wait.

"Alright, I gotta head out," John says, looking more exasperated than usual even. I've never pried into his business, but these days it's getting harder and harder to even imagine what it is he does. In this city, it could be anything, and I start seriously thinking about asking one of the other girls at the club if they'd like to split rent with me.

"Alright, I'll put some supper in the fridge for you," I call out as he goes. I'm too good to that man, for all the trouble he puts me through.

"Oh, one thing," John says, poking his head back in through the door. "If anyone comes looking for me… you don't know where I am," he says.

"That's easy, I never know where you are," I respond, a bit confused. But then it strikes me, how nervous he's acting, and the strange request. "Wait, what's going on?" I ask, suddenly getting a big afraid.

"Nothing. None of your business, I gotta go," he says, rushing off again, leaving me with a million questions and a very bad feeling in my gut.

Five years. Five years of my life gone.

That's about as much time as I spent in the marines. I don't like that line of thought. It crushes me. The marines defined who I was more than anything in my life besides my family. So what has prison done to me?

It has hardened me. Even more than fighting overseas, if I'm being honest. I expected to see certain things in combat. I knew I'd lose people. But we were allies working towards a common goal.

In prison, it was every man for himself, and I hated myself for the things I had to do, just to get out. Just to have the hope that on the other side, there was still something good that waited for me.

I didn't deny the charges in court. I merely stated my case as best I could. I told them what happened, and why I reacted as I did. I told them about my military service, and how much I fought and bled for my country.

But for that, I was sentenced to ten years. I got out with five on 'good behavior'.

Good behavior.

That's a joke.

Five years in a private prison, with other violent offenders. The food was shit. The guards treated us like shit. And we preyed on each other. Prison gangs ran things more than the prison administrators. Guards and prisoners working for thugs with connections on the outside.

Playing it good, doing my time and getting out was my goal. But how could I do that when I had multiple gangs pushing me to choose a side or get gutted by both?

In the end I did my best to stay out of the real fights, but I didn't come out clean.

I feel guilty, real guilty. But above it all, I feel bad about the woman I lost.

I never even got to tell Alice what happened. I never had her full name and address. She was staying in Vegas only temporarily — she said she was staying in a hotel. I never gave her my full name and I had no address, fresh from serving my stint in the marines.

I had no hope of tracking her down. Not unless she was still at that club, after all these years, and I know the career of most strippers is pretty short.

She would be long gone from there. Especially since her home was in Los Angeles, and she was just there for a brief stay.

She had dreams. She wanted to own her own little store. She wanted to raise a family. And the thought of her having moved on... it breaks my heart. I try not to think about what would happen if I find out she'd gotten engaged or married while I was locked up in a cell.

I can't let thoughts like that drag me down, though.

Leaving the prison, one of my last remaining wartime buddies picked me up. In good times, he's the last guy I'd turn to. He never came back from our time serving in Afghanistan and Iraq right. He couldn't hold down a regular job, and he fell in with the wrong crowd.

But where do I get off judging? At least he avoided prison. And for all his faults, his new 'friends' had connections in my prison that helped me get through without getting tangled up in anything too bad. Without having to do anything that risked my getting out on time.

"You should come work with me and the guys," he had offered on the car ride back. 'The guys' being his buddies, involved in all manners of crimes that I didn't want to get tangled up in.

I had told him 'no thanks', because I was planning on staying legit and seeing to my dreams. Same as always. I needed to put the past in the past, and move forward with my life.

Looking back, I feel like a fool.

Months of job searching, crashing on his couch, and what do I have to show for it? Endless rejections. Even in a city like Vegas, which is supposed to be the best spot in the country to come look for work.

But the best I got on offer was a job as at a grocery store. The owner offered to pay me under the table, because corporate wouldn't let him hire a guy with a criminal record. The pay was for less than minimum wage.

The job I was on my way to accepting before prison would've paid me $120,000 a year.

I'd be lucky to see that in a lifetime like this.

So one day, as I was getting ready to head out on another fruitless job search, my buddy comes to me in a fancy new suit. He's always coming back with some shiny new outfit or toy, but he never makes me feel bad for freeloading. He never needs to. My guilt eats at me every day, and I wonder if I shouldn't just take off out of Sin City.

But where would I go? I don't even have enough for a plane ticket.

"Hey, Vik," he says, "we need some help for something." He's anxious about asking me, I can tell right away. I've turned him down every time he asks, so it's no wonder.

But this time I listen. I listen because I'm desperate. Because living off of anyone's charity isn't my style. And that sleeping on my buddy's couch saps a bit more of my pride and my soul each day.

"There's this guy, right? A real piece of shit, trust me. He runs a sleazy brothel. Hurts the girls, ships 'em in from the Philippines away from their families to people who do God knows what to them. Well… we need to put the fear of God into him, if you know what I mean."

What am I supposed to say to that?

I'm avoiding the girls smoking as they watch the stage. I've been dancing for six years now, and dancer years are like dog years. I see the new girls come, hot as hell, expecting all the guys to give them their entire wallet just because they're sexy.

They quickly learn it doesn't work like that. To make money, it's not enough to look good. Hell, sometimes it doesn't take any looks at all. It takes customer service skills. You need to make the guy feel good.

I see their jealous eyes as I take man after man up to the VIP lounge, and I know the rumors they're spreading about me. They think I give blow jobs or full sex, but that's not true. I've only done anything beyond a good, clean dance with one customer, and I left the club for him.

I'm one of the cleanest dancers in this place, but I don't have a lot of friends to show for it. Though honestly, now that I'm in my early thirties and with a young kid to take care of, it doesn't bother me much. The newbies are all of twenty-two and half of them are only concerned with taking Instagram selfies in the dressing room. The others are like me, no matter their age. They're paying for college or kids, and we're in it to make money.

I appreciate their hustle, and they appreciate mine. Vaguely I wonder which of them I could trust enough to live with me and Cierra as I lead a well-dressed gentleman up to the VIP lounge. I go through the same old routine before ushering him into the private room. I smile, and I bring my fingers to my black bikini, and I wiggle my ass as he watches and hands me $20 bill after $20 bill.

Every single one, I mentally spend on Cierra, on rent, on groceries. Every winning smile I give him is going to give my baby girl a better life, and every time I moan in his ear, he's funding my kid's future education, whether he knows it or not.

Once his wallet is drained, I bring him down-stairs, and I kiss his cheek.

"Thank you, Anthony," I whisper in his ear. "Will I see you next month?"

He shakes his head sadly. "I'm away on business, but I'll be back in two with a big fat wad for you, Aphrodite," he promises, and I can't help but giggle.

"Oh Anthony, you always have a fat wad for me."

"I wish you'd come back to my place…" he trails off, but I shake my head, giving him a wink.

"You like me just where I am and you know it, sexy. Send me a text when you're back in town."

Just as the client is leaving, I hear a ruckus below. I peer out over the edge and see with my horror a few tough looking guys pushing around a bouncer. And that bouncer, Tom, is a big guy himself.

"Where is he, huh? Where is he?!" they shout at Tom, and as much as Tom is trying to remain tough and keep them back, he's outnumbered.

"I told you, John don't work here anymore," he says loudly. And my heart sinks.

John? They must mean… oh god. John. My ex-boyfriend.

We'd met here, he was a DJ, but he always had other things on the go. He said working here was more for fun and winked to me every time the topic of his work came up. I curse myself for being so stupid, for not seeing it sooner.

Then a while back he just quit entirely, didn't even do the part time work.

"Yeah well, we need to speak with John," shouts one of the thugs trying to intimidate Tom below. But the big bald brute of a bouncer holds his ground.

"I don't know where he's gone. Man just up and quit a while back," he insists, which is true enough. None of us knew the particulars of John's plans.

Why he quit, why he hasn't been around, or what he's doing now.

Even I don't know, not really, and he still lives with me. But suddenly I realize it's way bigger than what I could've possibly imagined. I thought maybe he was just working under the table, maybe has some petty scam on the go.

But petty scams don't get men like these shouting at bouncers in the middle of a busy strip club. These guys want to send a message.

"Well maybe one of these girls knows," the wire-thin but sadistic looking thug says, reaching out to grab one of the dancers. And my hackles raise; I don't want anyone to suffer for answers they don't have. And I very nearly shout out to leave her alone, to draw their attention to me, when Tom blocks them and protects the other dancer as she nervously scurries away.

"Ain't nobody here knows where he is, man! John ain't had many friends! He wasn't the type that was easy to like, you get what I'm sayin'? Wherever he is, ain't nobody here can help you," Tom insists. And for a moment it looks like the thugs aren't gonna be satisfied with that, that they're gonna beat the shit out of Tom. But they instead slowly back down.

"Well then. Guess we'll have to look elsewhere… for now. But if anyone knows where good ol' Johnny boy is," he flicks a card onto a table nearby. "Let us know, huh? 'Cause if we can't find him, we'll have to come knockin' on your door again."

What the hell has he gotten himself into now?

I'm not a dumb girl. I know that whatever he's got going on is going to blow back on me, and soon, and if someone finds out where he is, then they find out where I live.

Where Cierra lives.

VIKTOR

The corps trained me to fight with instinct; to act instead of think. Back home, that landed me in jail.

Yet here I am, parked outside a dingy 'foot spa' in a vehicle provided by my buddy. I know the risk I'm taking. This time, I'm risking jail not for a heat-of-the-moment lesson I wanted to teach a rapist. This time I have a record, and it's premeditated.

I turned down Mark's offer at first, but good ol' Mark talked me into it.

I have no options, and Mark knew just how to push me into this. He knew I couldn't say no to helping rescue some poor women from sex slavery. I know it happens, but now I know where to stop it.

I have nothing left to lose. I've looked for Alice, and she's moved on I guess. So all I have a dismal future making less than four dollars an hour under the table. I made more than that delivering papers as a boy, but now I can't even get a job like that again.

And at least here, I'll be able to make a difference. I'll be able to help people, doing what I do best.

I take the handgun from beneath the passenger seat and check it over. I can field strip one of these in little time, and I tell myself that going over the weapon will give me a moment to think this through.

Mark and I have been buddies for as long as we can remember. Mark's not even his real name; like me, his dad was another old Ukrainian emigre, and so he got the name Macario. But that was due for some Americanizing, and we shortened it to Mark over the years.

Our time serving had messed him up. He's involved in some criminal shit now, I know it. He's roped me into it, even. But I can't hold it against him. Not when I think back on the quiet, dorky kid he used to be. So kind, so giving. The sort of boy who'd give up his last dollar to another kid that didn't have a lunch.

I saw that kindness get beaten and tortured out of him, and now he's a jaded shell of the man he used to be.

It kills me to see him like he is now, but I'm still loyal to my friend. To the only friend I have left.

That's the thought that settles it. Instead of being dissuaded, I cock the gun and put it into the back of my jeans and get ready. I hope to God I don't need to use it, but there it is.

Heading into the dreary front door, it's not hard to immediately tell that this isn't a legitimate operation. There are cars parked out front, obviously clients, yet there's no foot massages or bathing going on up front. Just a couple of big, thuggish guys hanging out who eye me up and down for trouble.

"Can we help you?" the lone little woman that acts as the customer service rep asks.

"I'm here to see Zheng," I say, the name of the owner. Just saying that gets the backs of the two guys up.

"What do you wanna see him for?" one of them demands of me, a hand hovering near an undoubtedly hidden gun.

"He's done wrong by some people. I'm here to set him straight," I say, exactly what I was told to.

It's apparently also the secret code to make them turn violent, because the guy goes for his gun and I spring to action.

There's a couple feet between us, and I grab his wrist before he can pull out his gun and shatter his nose with a blow from my hand. The other guy comes at me with a knife, and it's only by pulling the other guys arm out that I'm able to shield myself from the stab, instead letting it sink into the forearm of the thug I'd just bludgeoned.

I head-butt him then quickly, breaking his nose

too as the little woman screams and runs away out the front door. It's just as well she gets out of here, this place won't be safe. It's already not safe.

I beat the two of them down and take their weapons, helping myself to the knife and a second gun.

"Get the fuck outta here if you don't wanna die," I growl at them before heading towards the back room.

Part of me says I shouldn't let them live. That these are some criminal thugs that'll just get me in the back when I move on. Same as what landed me in jail. I was lucky then; the bullet didn't penetrate my thick skull. It just really fucked me up and left me for the police to collect and charge.

I push on, up the stairs and into the back of the operation.

There's a guy watching the door and he has a gun, which leaves me little option. I pull mine and order him to drop it. He looks surprised I even asked, takes a moment to consider whether he'll try and point his gun at me. But thinks better of it.

"Drop it," I order him again, and he does. I jerk my head to the side, "Go. Get out of here."

He hesitates but then takes off, letting me carry on through the door.

But I'm not prepared for what I find on the other side.

This isn't any brothel that might be legally run outside the city, regardless of how shitty they might be. This is sex slavery. Women, some of whom are chained up and clearly unwilling, being abused by men.

I knew what this was a front for, but I didn't expect it to be so blatant. So heinous. The fact that there are men willing to see women who are crying and hurting...

I start to see red, but there's too many. Even though they're almost all clients, I can't just start beating them all down.

My finger twitches. I wanna kill them all. Not beat them. These are men that deserve to die. Not like the brave friends and soldiers I lost overseas. We fought for their freedoms and this is how they use it, to torture those weaker than them.

I have killed men, plenty of men, just because my commanding officer told me. Just because my country asked it of me.

What's any less wrong about killing these pieces of scum?

But the thought doesn't complete before I realize I made my way to the back door. My legs had kept moving, despite my inner turmoil, and I'm at the boss's office, exactly where Mark told me it'd be. It's wide open, and a little bald man sits behind the desk, with the largest thug yet standing by his side. A bodyguard probably.

Suddenly all my reason for being here seems to matter so little.

This shithead endangered some criminal operation by smuggling in Filipino women through the ships that bring in drugs and guns. The other crime bosses don't care that he's a sex trafficker, a slaver. They just want him to stop putting their less-reviled operations at risk.

They want me to scare the shit out of this guy. Or end his business. Those were Mark's words.

And he didn't sound like he cared too much if I just ended it.

I hear a scream behind me, one of the women. I turn around, thinking maybe she saw the gun I was holding, but it's not me she was screaming about. It's that guy at the door I told to scram. He came back.

And he fires at me.

Thankfully my training had kicked in instantly, and I was already throwing myself out of the way before he pulled that trigger. There's no outrunning bullets once they're on their way, after all. He misses, but I don't.

Right in the forehead. He's down.

But I missed the element of surprise. The guys in the room know I'm here now. Women are screaming, men are screaming, clients in stages of undress are rushing out.

Crouched to the ground, I roll across the office door length, unbothered by the screams. I lived through far worse than this, performed under more dangerous circumstances than this organization has available to them.

The guard fires at me as he crouches behind the desk. He misses with my movement, but I don't. I hit his ankle beneath the desk, which causes him to fall forward. His head's my next target.

My hesitation has nearly cost me everything tonight, but I'm in fighting mode. Headshots are what I'm after. That's what I was trained for. Marines aren't police; we're not trained to disable. We're trained to kill and get the job done.

And if ever there was a more righteous cause than this, I don't know of it.

Another thug comes running out of a side door and I pop one in his skull before he can even see me on the floor.

I pause, listen. The screams fade. The running of feet heading away recede. I don't hear anymore coming. That must be it.

Of all the people I killed — enemy soldiers, terrorists — this balding prick has it coming the most I figure. He didn't do this because he believes in anything. He enslaved and brutalized women not for a cause, but because he's a greedy prick. Because he can.

So I make my move into the office. The pudgy little bald man has a gun, but he doesn't know how to use it. I do.

I end him and think not another thing about it. He's not worth it. I go to his pockets and quickly find a set of keys. I take them into my gloved hands, and swiftly move to one of the chained up women. I put my gun back against my spine, safety on, and show her I mean no harm before I quickly unlock her.

I hand her the keys and she heads to the next woman with trembling hands. They're taking care of each other. Even though she could run, she spends the precious time unlocking each of the other women, and that helps heal my heart a little from what I've just seen.

I head out. I gotta go before the cops get here.

I don't feel bad for what I did. None of these guys had the slightest shred of decency if they were willing to stand by and watch this shit happen. I only regret not killing those fuckers I first saw, and putting my life in danger for no reason.

Part of me asks: what am I becoming?

Nothing worse than what I already was, I tell myself.

was pretty shaken up by the events at the club, Tom — the bouncer — told me that he had my back, that he wasn't gonna tell some thugs where I or anyone was. And I believe he meant it, but it's hard to know what a man will do when put to the knife.

Tom and I have been friends ever since we moved to a new club together. I think we both needed a change, though he was always so stoic, and I never asked why he wanted out of the last club. For me, it was that memories of Viktor never stopped coming and after a while, I had to move on. After I took a leave of absence for my pregnancy, I wanted a new start.

I wanted a place that wouldn't constantly remind me of how hard and fast my feelings for Viktor had started, and how much my heart ached when he didn't show up. It had taken my business attitude about work and destroyed it.

So I trust that Tom is telling the truth. We've been through a lot together already. But eventually, those men are going to find out where John is.

If it were just me, I might not let it get to me so much. I'd stick my chin out and put on a tough act, but there's Cierra to worry about now. Motherhood changes the whole equation for me, I've learned.

This club is a bit more upper class, with a wealthier client base. It even helped my earnings a bit to move, to be the new girl at a different club. But that wanes fast, and it inevitably comes down to your hustle.

Stripping is a sales job at its core, all about your hustle. The most beautiful women on the planet can go into a strip club with all the confidence in the world, but if they don't have the hustle and the personality, they'll walk away with very little money. You learn fast that the most piggish, superficial men have more standards than even they think and don't part with money without some style and skill behind your game.

But now I'm wondering if maybe I shouldn't move again. Go to a new club, disappear. Maybe that would help protect me from those thugs.

I'm spending tonight in hiding, texting various

clients and letting them know I'm only available by special request, but when my eyes glance up from my phone, I see a face I never thought I'd see again.

Viktor's.

After all these years… it nearly floors me. Quite literally, as I almost topple over on my stilettos in shock. He's like a ghost of the past. A walking apparition. He's still just as handsome, though he's a bit older now and more rugged.

I never thought I'd see him again. I'd thought of hiring a detective a few times to track him down, to let him know he has a little girl. But if he didn't care enough to stick around, I didn't want to rope him back in. And besides, I had so little to go on. All I knew that was concrete was his first name and the knowledge he grew up in some little coastal town in Maine.

I didn't think it'd be enough for even a seasoned investigator.

But after five years, I find myself staring in shock.

He's dressed up nicely, in a suit. It looks too warm for a Vegas tourist; none of them ever tolerate a full suit for long. My own intuition tells me he's been in the area for a while. More so because he's not here on a visit, that much is clear. He's marching back towards the office to speak with the manager, like a man on a mission.

Curiosity gets the better of me, and I peer after him, watch him slip in back. One of the bouncers I don't know the name of tries to shut the door on Viktor, but he doesn't let them. He keeps it open, and though I can't hear the words that transpire between them I can tell he's being threatening.

It's unreal. Sure, it's not the screaming match with the thugs, but it's clear that Viktor is putting the fear of god into them.

I watch as the manager throws up his hands, seems to curse, but ultimately hands over several stacks of bills, stuffing it into a black satchel that Viktor has.

Is he with some local gang? My heart sinks... What has happened to him in these past five years? What type of man has he become?

But I'm so wrapped up in the moment, in the pang I feel in my heart, that I'm too slow to move out of sight when he turns to leave and he catches sight of me.

My heart jumps into my throat and I want to bolt.

But it's too late. Our eyes lock.

It feels like the moment drags on forever, but it must be no more than a heartbeat before I tear myself away and try to head off. I can't face him. I can't hear why he abandoned me. All these years, I've come up with stories I told myself when I couldn't sleep. That he enlisted for a second tour;

that he left. That he got a great job offer and couldn't wait. That he's off somewhere living a happy life without me.

Or that I was just a dumb stripper who gave him a free night of fun and he bragged about it to all his buddies before forgetting I existed.

I can't face the potential that the last story was right. The shame and embarrassment of falling in love with someone who doesn't even think of you is too much.

"Alice! Alice!" he calls as I try to head away, but the crowd is thick and I know it's futile. More than that, some anger boils up in me, from him having taken off long ago without showing up for our date.

"Stop letting everyone know my real name," I turn and mutter to him in irritation.

He freezes right before me, looking me over like I was a ghost.

"Sorry," he says right away, running a hand back over his sleek wheat-blonde hair. "I just... I didn't know if you heard me."

It's all happening too fast, and I don't have time to sort through the whirlwind of emotions that's brewing in my heart. I never thought I'd see him again, and I'd long ago given up on finding him. Yet here he is, walking back into my club, and looking at me like...

Like what? Like he's surprised. Happy, even. But then, I guess he should be. Maybe he thinks this'll be round two, enough time passed between us that a second one-night-stand might be in order.

And who knows what extortion racket he's involved with now. I knew military guys had a tough time transitioning back into the civilian population, but I didn't take him to be the guy caught up in that crap.

"It's Aphrodite," I remind him, and part of me wants to storm away, never hearing his excuses for why he didn't show up. I don't want him to charm me again, and I know if he smiles at me, my heart is going to leap out of my chest with joy.

I didn't think love at first sight was supposed to last through heartbreak. How can I still feel so strongly for a man I only spent a few hours with? Tears are threatening my eyes, but I can't allow them to spill. I can't show him how much I missed him.

How much I still miss him.

"Aphrodite," he repeats after me, like that name is precious to him too. He wets his lips, "Look, I—" he looks like he's about to offer me some excuses, but thinks better of it. Maybe it's the look on my face, or maybe it's just that he's smarter than the average man and knows better than to try, but he drops it. "I've thought about you a lot," he says instead.

"That's nice," I say, and it breaks my heart to be so cold to him. This isn't how I wanted it to go. I dreamed of seeing him again, of hearing his voice and feeling his touch. In the dark of the night, it was always him my mind went back to.

I pictured running into him on the street, seeing him light up and tell me how wrong he was to abandon me. Some romantic version of love that doesn't exist.

And now he's here, back in my life like a fantasy come to life, and I don't even know where to begin, so I glance down at his bag. "I guess you got what you came here for, huh?"

Viktor had strut in here looking fierce and intimidating, but when I said that, he looks down at the satchel full of money and seems full of shame. It was the most complete reversal I'd ever seen in a man in such a short amount of time.

"I guess so," he says, sounding a little defeated. "I… I didn't want us to meet like this again. I mean… I never thought I could find you again. I checked the club over and over, and you weren't there. Not that I thought it's likely you'd still be around. I thought you might have gone back home in LA," he says.

"Things changed pretty fast after that night," I say with a shrug, letting him read into that what he would.

"They did," he says with an air of resignation. "Look, I know you don't owe me anything… and I have a lot of explaining to do, but…" he rubs at his lightly stubbled jaw. "Let me take you dinner and try to make things right. A proper date," he offers, that confidence and charm I knew long ago eroded away, replaced by his apologetic demeanor.

It was such a change. Five years ago, he acted like the world was at his feet. He was happy and excited, ready to start anew. Now he was jaded, beaten down by reality, and that crushed me.

But then, I was beaten down by reality too. Raising my baby girl — his child — on my own had taken a toll. I replaced my dreams with hers, and funded them with a career I thought I'd only be in for a couple of years.

I glance around at the club, trying to buy time. I don't know what a date with him with look like. Not anymore.

"I'm not available at night," I respond honestly. "Or... days." That part was true too. Cierra wouldn't be in school until next year, and she doesn't have a regular sitter, especially now that the school year was back in session.

My rejection saddens him; I can see it even though he hides it well, and it hurts my heart. But he gives me a nod.

"Of course," he says respectfully. Whatever he's become since my one-night stand with him, he still honors my wishes. "I wish I hadn't screwed things up for us. But I just want you to know that I regret daily that I did," he says. "Good luck Alice. I hope life gives you nothing but roses," he says as he turns and walks on out of my life again.

I can already feel the tears running down my cheeks, and I angrily swat them away. I draw in my lower lip and pray my mascara doesn't run.

But my heart is breaking as I let him walk away. I've just thrown away my only chance at true love. At the one man who could make my home a family.

The only man I've ever really loved.

I blew my chance with Alice long ago. That's the truth of it. No matter how right it might've been to lay a beat down on that piece of shit rapist, it cost me my chance with the only woman that really ever had my heart.

I try to tell myself that it was a one night fling, that it likely would've gone nowhere anyhow. But I don't believe it, not in my heart.

She was still just as beautiful, but she looked a bit wiser now. More confident in that invisible way. I wanted her just as badly seeing her again as I did that first night, but so much has changed. I shouldn't have wanted to bring her back into my life now anyways. What kind of life could I offer a woman like that?

Instead I try to focus on my job. Mark is here, pointing out the building.

"Look, there's a guy that owes us a ton of money," he says to me.

"No shit. They all do, that's why you send me," I tell him. I know the job enough by now to know that almost every time, that's the reason I'm sent out. Some piece of shit low-level criminal owes them money. It's not as satisfying as the first job he sent me on, to bust up that slave trading piece of shit Zheng, but I don't feel bad about busting in the face of a guy who robs grocers and liquor stores either.

"No no, you see, the problem this time is that he doesn't just owe us. Normally we only lend to a guy if we know we're his only creditors, but this time it turns out he secretly owed a bunch to some other folks too. Including some Chinese mobsters. You know the ones, same type who ran that place you busted up on your first night," Mark explains to me.

"Yeah, hard to forget," I tell him. And it is. Not because I feel bad; nobody I shot or beat down didn't have it coming.

But because it was the start of my new criminal life. And the start of finally making some serious money. Enough to live like a real man who might be going somewhere someday. If I can keep it up for a few more years, I might even be able to get rid of my prison record and find some honest work.

"So we need you to track him down and collect before they do. He owes us a lot here, bud," he stresses to me needlessly. "If they get to him first, they'll wring him dry and we'll not get a penny, ya dig?"

"Yeah I got it," I tell him a bit more impatiently than I intend. I don't like what Mark does — what we do — but I shouldn't take it out on him. He's had a hard life from beginning to now. What he does — what we do, I remind myself again — isn't right, but I am in no place to judge. "I'm on it, so it's as good as done," I assure him.

"That's the Vik I know," he says to me with a broad grin and a slap on my shoulder. And with that, I'm off.

It's not a ritzy high-end place my trail leads me to, however. It's not even a house. It's a pretty simple, working class apartment complex. Nice and safe, but not expensive. It's not what I expect when tracking down a deadbeat criminal bum, but since it's his last known whereabouts, I'll take it.

When I get there though, I notice something out of place. There's one expensive black mustang, parked haphazardly in the lot. Like some rich prick who doesn't care about his vehicle getting damaged by another driver — not likely in this neighborhood — or someone in a real hurry.

Either way, this hints I'm on the right track.

I climb the outdoor stairs towards the apartment on the second floor, taking my gun in hand just in case. My time in the marines and doing this job have taught me many things and one point where they cross over is this: I don't take chances. And I can't afford pity for my enemies. Pity gets me killed in both worlds; or at least in civilian life, it puts me back in prison.

My target's apartment door is open, as in wide open. I approach with caution, pulling my gun out of my jacket entirely. But then I hear something that causes me to throw all caution to the wind.

"Don't touch my daughter!" a woman cries. But I recognize that voice. I recognize it all too well.

It's Alice.

I grab my stiletto heel that was lying beside the closet, and I charge at the man nearest me. I don't have a thought, not a single fear going through my mind. It's all adrenaline. The second that man touched my daughter, I was seeing red. My stiletto heel nailed his shoulder, and his grip slackened on Cierra.

"Go to your room!" I tell her, as I strike for him again, the high heel aimed this time for his face. There's so much fury behind my actions, and I'm sure they didn't expect it from me. I'm still in my pink pajamas, my hair pulled back in a loose bun, and mascara rings still under my eyes from all the crying I'd done this morning before Cierra woke up.

But all my heartbreak is forgotten, and the only thing on my mind is protecting her.

These two guys are big though, and I'm not sure

even a mother's fury could overpower one of them, let alone both. I attack the guy before me all the same; it doesn't matter that I might lose, that I might die, I just need to beat this guy down and then worry about the rest later. My daughter depends on it.

"You fucking whore!" he cries at me, punching me with the weight of an anvil, but I just keep attacking. I stab the heel of my stiletto into his shoulder and he cries out, the heel lodged in his flesh as he reels back. I don't give in, and I claw at his eyes, push him back.

I've done so much for my girl. I gave up my dreams of owning and running a little bookstore and coffee shop, I've danced every night of the week for as long as I could handle it to pay for her future. I'll fight these guys down, I'll do it. I'll make it happen. And I dig my thumbs into this man's eyes, my nails breaking but the jagged pieces digging in all the same and making him scream out.

Nobody fucks with my daughter!

I break him down as he cries in pain, his muscles going to little use as he tries to pull my arms away from him, but it's too late. I'm lodged in there, and no force on earth is going to make me back off.

And then he goes slack. I feel crazed, but I'm a mom now. And I'm only half done.

I look at the other guy, ready for blood. But he's got a gun out. And suddenly reality floods back in: I'm going to die.

I could have strength enough to lift a bus, but a bullet will still end me.

I scream and get ready to attack him too, all the same. But the bang of a gun going off resonates and…

He slumps to the ground, lifeless.

I'm confused. Bloodied. But mainly confused.

Then I look to the door.

The last person I ever expected to see again.

Viktor. Standing there. Gun out. He'd shot the thug once in the back of the head, but didn't wait, he moved to the guy I attacked. Then put a bullet in his head too, just in case.

"Is that all of them?" he asks me, sounding all business. Like a soldier.

"Yes," I say, but my world is spinning, my arms shaking wildly. What have I done? What's going on?

I have two corpses in my living room, and he's standing in front of me like out of a dream. Is this heaven? Have I died, and now I'm just seeing the man I love, one final time? Hallucinating our victory before I pass over?

"Are you okay?" he steps up to me, placing a hand on my cheek, looking into my eyes. But it's not a romantic gaze, as much as my first impulse is to see it as one. He's checking me out like it's a battlefield, trying to see if I'm hurt. "Where's your daughter? Is she safe? I heard you cry out about her," he explains.

"Cierra," I whisper, before bolting from Viktor

towards her room. I open her door, and I don't see her at first. But then I see the closet is a little ajar, and I cautiously open it, finding my little girl's terrified face staring at me.

Tears are already streaming down my face as I open my arms for her hug. "It's okay. They're gone," I coo in her ear, rocking her as she cries into my shoulder.

Viktor enters the room a little while later, looking so serious, all business. I can't tell if it's the gangster or the soldier in him.

"Is she okay? If so, we should go. This place won't be safe. They won't be the last," he says to me, as if this all makes sense. As if two thugs showing up out of nowhere, demanding to know where John is, was somehow all normal, expected stuff that he was prepared to handle.

I cover her ears as I look back at him. "This is our home. I can't just... just... take her somewhere else. There is nowhere else."

"Come to my place," he tells me. "It's new, it's nice, there's room for you both. I'll protect you and your daughter," he says to me with such conviction and certainty. "But whatever you do, we can't wait. Trouble is going to be here any moment now, one way or another. We really need to go, Alice."

I'm about to argue, but I know, in part, he's right. At least going with the devil I know will buy me some time to figure out where to go. I go to my side dresser and take out a small stack of bills, then rush into the kitchen. In the back of the oven's drawer, I take out three envelopes: everything I'd saved for Cierra's future. No one knew about this money. Not even John. Especially not John. I tuck it in my purse, and quickly pack an overnight bag.

"We're going to spend the night with mommy's friend," I tell Cierra in her room, as I grab some clothes for her. "But first, we gotta play hide and go seek." I hold out a blindfold, and though she looks at me skeptically, she lets me tie the black fabric around her eyes. "I'll just carry you outside and we'll play at his place!"

She's unsure and confused, but I manage to assure her and get her to go along with it as Viktor escorts us out. He peers outside like it's some kind of action movie, but after what I just lived through, I'm convinced it's necessary.

He takes me on down to his car, a nice but simple black ride, and he opens the door for Cierra and me in the back.

"Won't be long and we'll chill out at my place, you two," he tells us, speaking in a reassuring tone for Cierra. And instantly he's hopping into the driver seat and starting up. I worry for a moment he'll tear out of there like a bat out of hell and freak her out, but he's both speedy and safe, taking his time.

I can hear sirens and I start to panic.

"Viktor…" I say, tension high in my voice.

"Don't worry, Alice," he tells me, driving away calmly as if nothing is wrong. The cop cars racing by, undoubtedly on their way to my place after reports of gunfire. But they pay us no mind, and we head on down the road at a casual driving pace.

My heart is pounding so hard in my chest, but I slump back in my seat, cradling Cierra to my chest, rocking her back and forth gently. She knows something is wrong. She's a smart kid, and she can feel the tension in my bones. But I can't do anything about that. All I can do is feel relieved that she's safe.

Viktor glances back at us in the rearview mirror and smiles handsomely, just like I knew he could.

"Don't worry ladies. You'll love my place. It's almost fit for two lovely queens like yourselves," he says in that disarming way of his. "How about I treat you both to some pizza when we get there, huh? I know a great place, you'll love it. If you're a good girl they even bring you some fresh baked cookie pie."

"Would you like that, Cierra?" I ask her, and even though she's shy and likely terrified, she nods her head eagerly. "Tell Viktor," I urge her.

"I'd like that," she says in a soft voice, and I kiss the crown of her head.

Though now that the adrenaline has faded, I catch Viktor's eyes in the mirror.

Does he know that she's his?

My new apartment has barely been broken in before I bring my two new guests over. It's furnished lightly, with a stylish living room set, TV and sound system. My bedroom has a large king-sized bed, and while I turned one of the spare rooms into a workout room, the third sits unused.

I welcome them both in, carrying Cierra for Alice as I point to the washroom so she can clean the blood off of her.

"Hey now, Cierra," I say to the young girl with a smile, "I don't have a lot of toys around here, but I tell you what… I'll order your favorite kind of pizza and treat you like a princess as long as you're in my castle, how's that sound?" I ask her before putting her down on a chair, like she was a queen taken upon a palanquin to her throne.

She's had a long day, so I don't blame her for the way she looks at me with that curious expression, and those big, green eyes. Her head tilts to the side, her curly blonde hair gone a bit matted against her head from the blindfold. After a few seconds of thinking about it, her eyes darting to the bathroom where her mom had gone, she nods and gives me a small smile.

"Like Prince Charming," she says, her speech remarkably good for a four-year-old.

"Well, I won't say I'm all that charming, but you're welcome to Prince Charming's castle," I say with a smile and a wink. I place the order, take a while to hang out with the young girl. She reminds me so much of Alice, but in a mini, childlike version.

I haven't spent any time with kids in years, but luckily it turns out the fancy new TV I bought came with a games console, and I introduced her to Minecraft on it, buying Alice the time she needs to not only clean but to cope with all that's happened. I don't expect any of this to be easy for her.

Most of my mind is screaming at me to go check up on Alice, to make sure she's okay. But I know that as a mom — a tenacious mom I saw in action, at that — her first concern would be for her girl. So I shove down my own worries, my selfish concerns for the love I lost, and do my best to keep young Cierra happy. Comforting Alice would be more for me than her; comforting her daughter is the most selfless thing I can do.

And she seems like a really happy kid. Now that she feels a bit safer, I can see her opening up, giggling and laughing. But every once in a while a strange look comes over her as she looks at me, like she's trying to figure me out. I guess it's just having someone new around, especially after the type of day she had.

But then she smiles, and those dimples show in her cheeks as she turns back to the TV, or towards the door.

"Mommy never lets me have pizza," she confides, and for a second I wonder if I did something wrong. But Alice never mentioned anything in the car, so I guess it's more of a personal preference than an allergy.

Cierra starts climbing on me, and I spread my legs to let her get cozy between them, both of us sitting casually on the floor, my back against the sofa. She didn't seem to care for sitting on the couch, but she seems to warm right up to using me as her backrest.

"So how old are you now, Cierra?" I ask, and she puts up four fingers, beaming proudly at me. "I'm almost four-and-a-half," she boasts, and I can't help but smile. Her beguiling smile is infectious, especially as she rests her head on my stomach, looking at me upside down.

"That's so old," I say, my eyes going wide, my tone teasing, and she laughs at me, her head shaking, golden curls going wild.

"Not as old as mommy. Or you," she adds, and I grin.

"How old do you think mommy is?"

"Real old. This many," she says, holding up nine fingers, and I laugh as I capture them in my hands.

"Wow, that is old," I tease, and she laughs, squirming in my lap before heading for the door. I don't know what she's after, but just then the door-bell rings. Kid must have a sixth sense for timing.

I open the door and tip the pizza guy before taking a glance around. I know no one saw me leave, but it doesn't hurt to be cautious.

Cierra makes grabby hands at the pizza, dessert, salads and drinks as I move into the kitchen, rebuking her with a grin. "We have to wait for your mom," I remind her, and she lets out an exasperated sigh.

"She's always in there forever with makeup," she says, then pouts, "and never lets me wear any."

"You want to be like mommy?"

"Mhm," she says with an adamant nod, and I grin, stroking her hair.

"She's pretty great," I agree. "But so are you," I say as I pick her up, and she happily laughs into my shoulder as I zoom her about the apartment.

I pass the time with the girl some more, but still Alice isn't out.

"Y'know what, your mom wants you to be a growing girl more than anything. So I'm sure this once time she'll forgive you for starting without her," I say with a wink, opening the box of pizza and handing her a slice. "How's that?"

She cries out excitedly, taking the slice and biting into it with a big smile. I like the girl, I realize. She's so much like her mom, it's endearing in every way. And we get along so naturally.

But our pleasant moment gets disrupted by a crash from the hallway.

I shed some more tears, this time not over lost love but the frantic hell that my life became so suddenly. Or maybe not so suddenly. I was just so busy with taking care of Cierra and working, I didn't realize what John was pulling me into.

My daughter nearly saw that gruesome display, my life turned upside down, and now I'm staying in the hands of a man I barely know. A killer.

But my hands have blood on them too. Did I kill that man when I shoved my thumbs into his eyes? I don't know. Not for sure.

It's gut-wrenching. And just when I think I'm ready to head out and join them, I peek my head out of the hall quietly, and see them…

Viktor, for all his faults, is sat there, playing games with my daughter — our daughter — as if she were his own. His charming smile back in full force, his natural good nature easing her tensions, making her happy.

He doesn't look like a thug or a gangster. He looks like the man I fell deeply in love with. The man I shared my dreams and passions with as he held me for that one perfect night.

I feel the tears welling back up and I head into the bathroom again a while. When I next emerge I see them chatting, him handing her a slice of pizza. And it's so touching. He doesn't know it's his daughter, but he's so kind. So fatherly all the same.

A dizzy spell comes over me and I stumble, knocking a picture off the wall and it hits the floor with a crash.

Viktor goes for his gun, hidden beneath his blazer. But he sees it's me quickly and relaxes.

"Alice," he sighs with relief, and luckily Cierra didn't see the gun he hid. "Just in time to join us for the pizza," he says, serving me up a slice on a paper plate.

"Prince Charming, mama!" she says, and I wish she hadn't. I guess some part of those stories I told her about my waylaid love life remained somewhere in her memories.

"It smells delicious," I say, avoiding her comment with a smile as I slide into my seat. I've scrubbed my face, and I'm sure it's red and puffy, and my hair is still tied back in a bun. I wanted to take a shower, but I wasn't ready to be naked. Not yet. That was a level of vulnerability I'm not prepared for.

I thought about texting John, some dumb sense of loyalty welling up inside me, but he nearly got my girl killed. He's the one that put this blood on my hands, and he doesn't deserve the courtesy of knowing what type of people are after him. As if he doesn't know already.

Not just that, but being in contact with him would only put us at greater risk. I don't know who he's in deep with, but it's no one I want to tangle with.

"And make sure to save room, there's dessert after," Viktor says with a wink to Cierra, her eyes going wide. The next while goes by so quickly, so naturally. I couldn't have anticipated that we'd all just mesh so well as a little unit.

A family.

Before I know it, Cierra — and Viktor — are guiding me to the couch, to show me what she's created in the game. The three of us sitting there, laughing and smiling. And it's almost like none of the horrors of the day occurred.

Night scarcely seems to have set when Cierra falls asleep on the couch, and we quietly make our getaway to another room.

"Are you okay?" he asks me when the door's barely been shut a half-second. There is a look of concern on his handsome, rugged face.

"I am definitely not okay," I answer honestly. "What the hell were you doing at my apartment? Because stalking is really not the way to win me back." All that anger and fear that I'd pushed down for my daughter's sake is coming bubbling to the surface.

"I wasn't stalking you," he says in an even, patient voice. "I was looking for a man who owed a friend of mine a lot of money. I was trying to get to him before some other, nastier folk got to him first. Clearly, I was too slow."

"Jesus," I reply, my hand going to my forehead. How many people are after John? He's in way deeper than I thought...

I slump back against the wall, the wind taken out of my sails. "What'd your friend say about him?"

"Just..." he hesitates, and I can tell immediately that he's trying to soften the blow. "That he's tangled up in some very bad things. That he's done some stuff he shouldn't have. Really shouldn't have. And that I was supposed to get to him while there was still someone to get to." He takes in a deep breath, his broad shoulders rising up, his chest swelling. "I had no idea you're going out with him."

"I'm not," I say, maybe a little too quickly. "He's my deadbeat ex who refused to move out after I dumped him. And he's been shifty as hell lately, so this explains a lot."

He looks a little stunned, relieved? It's hard to tell, but he nods.

"Good. I mean, it's good you're not still tangled up with a man that's tied up in this shit," he says, a sort of melancholy falling over him for a moment. "I am so sorry for everything, Alice. But I will find a way to return you to your life, and solve all of this. I promise."

"They were hassling girls at the club. Threatening them to try to find out where John was. I couldn't tell them, and if they come back, looking for blood... Oh God, Viktor, what if they screw with the club? What if they find out that I knew him? If he's really in as deep as you say," I sob, completely losing my cool once more, tears streaming down my face. "I didn't even know what he was into."

Viktor's fists clench and then unclench, his hands going to my shoulders to hold me comfortingly.

"I never wanted to get tangled up in any of this," he says to me in that deep, husky voice of his. "But now that I am, I can help you, Alice. I'll make sure these men don't bother you or your coworkers again, you hear me?" He looks me in the eyes so dead serious, so certain. "I never got to make our date five years ago. And as much as that pains me, it was for a good reason. And it's the same reason I'm going to go and finish these fuckers for you tonight. I'm going to make sure they can't hurt you or anyone like you, you hear me?"

Hurt lances my heart as I look at him through blurry eyes. This was the man I always wanted to be with, the one I longed for.

But I don't know how deep this goes. Whatever he's into...

"I feel like I don't know you at all," I admit, another sob coming from my chest. "You told me so much, but you never... you never told me who you really were."

"But I did," he says without hesitation, looking a bit pained. "Or at least as much as I could." He runs a hand back over his hair again with frustration. "I wasn't tangled up in any of this that night. Every-thing..." he struggles and I don't know what he wants to say but feels unable to. "Everything went to shit right before our date. I made a stupid mistake. And I paid five years of my life for it in prison. Five fucking years. More than I spent in the corps," he says, his broad jaw jutting out as he fought his anger. "I didn't have your name, your full name, I didn't have any way to tell you it all. And... frankly, I didn't want to drag you into my fucked up life after I was arrested anyhow. You didn't deserve that bullshit hanging over your head."

The charming, handsome knight was replaced by a pained, embittered man. That made him all the more real and endearing in some ways until his words sink in.

"You were arrested? You were in prison?" I can't

believe the shock that goes through me, and all the food in my stomach churns, threateningly. All those years, I was thinking of him just getting cold feet, being a charming playboy... Never in my wildest fantasies...

"I know, I know," he says, scratching at his scalp, tousling his handsome blonde hair. "I never thought that'd be the kind of man I'd become. But… well," he licked his lips, "fuck it. What's it matter? I did it and I served my time. But I never stopped thinking about you. Even though I knew I didn't deserve you anymore. Fuck, I couldn't even find a real job when I got out. How was I supposed to win over a woman like you?"

He says that like I'm the finest woman he's ever met.

Like he still pined for me the way I pined for him.

Fresh tears spring to my eyes, and all I want to do is fall into him once more. To forget this horrible day in his body, and just let myself feel something other than heartbreak and fear. I wanted to be weak, if only for a little while, and I stare into his eyes for what feels like a long time.

"What did you do," I manage, but I'm afraid to find out. But not knowing... How can I trust him with Cierra and me without knowing?

"I beat a guy up. Bad," he says to me. "I was coming to visit you just as you got off work, when I saw..." his fists clench. "Well, some piece of shit was harassing a dancer. I couldn't let it go. It got ugly," he says. "She got away and went back into the club. But I was shot, arrested and convicted. Rich son of a bitch wasn't gonna let me get away with beating the crap out of him."

"Jesus, Viktor," I curse, swiping my tears away. "Jesus," I repeat as it slowly dawns on me. I'd seen Julie in the dressing room, fighting with one of the new dancers around that time. I thought it was strange, since Julie was usually sweeter than pie. And I knew she'd been having trouble with a rich guy she'd been seeing. She mentioned having a date with him, but he'd invited some friends and things got brutal. She didn't dance for very long after that.

But I'd never even heard about the trial. I guess I was distracted with feeling betrayed Viktor at the time…

"I know. I know, Alice," he says with a sigh. "It's not what I had banked on for my life, that's for sure. And it's certainly not what's right for you. I've got no illusions of this leading us back together. As much as I'd love to be in yours and your girl's life, I've fucked things up too much for that now. But I will fix things for you. I'll set it all straight before you leave. On my honor," he says with such grim determination.

My eyebrows furrow in confusion.

"You haven't figured it out?"

"Figured out what?" he asks me, his stern brow knit as he stares at me. He has no idea.

I shake my head and sigh. Do I even tell him? I always thought I would, if the chance ever came. Just to let him know. To let him be fair. And he looked like such a natural with her. If he didn't even realize that she was his, then clearly he has... something in him. Some fatherly connection that he doesn't realize is even there.

He's also a killer, I argue with myself. But then... so am I. Whether I finished him with my thumbs or not, am I really that much better? We're both on the run from the law, whether I like that or not. And it was all to protect Cierra. It was justified.

I lick my lips.

"What is it, Alice?" he asks me again, his voice lower, more tender as he rubs my arms. "You don't need to worry. I'll die to protect you and Cierra, if that's what it takes. On what honor I have left as a veteran of the corps, I'll not let you and that little girl down. If there's one last thing I can do in this life that's right and just, it'll be to free you from the thugs that are out to ruin your life."

"Viktor... do you remember what happened that night between us?"

He pauses for a moment before cracking a smile.

"There's not a moment of that night I haven't etched in my memory forever. From the time I first saw you on stage, to the moment we realized we were talking well past sun up. And everything in between, like—" and then it dawns on him. His eyes widening. "She's not… really?" he says, and at first I think he's mortified, but then I see it spreading across his face. A look of joy I've never expected to see on a man's face after giving him that kind of news. "I've got a daughter…?" he says, and right before me that big-hearted brute of a marine began to look glassy-eyed.

I nod.

There's no words, not really. Nothing that can convey the emotions I feel rising up in my heart, in my throat, all threatening to take my over. I can't even pick them out as they swirl together, just giving me this warm but mournful feeling in my chest.

"I guess we're both just that good," I finally manage through my tightened throat.

He looks back at the door, as if he's going to run out and grab Cierra up and hug her right now. But he thinks better of it, looks back to me and cracks a smile, laughing softly as he grabs a hold of me and squeezes me tightly in his arms.

"Fuck Alice, I can't believe I missed out on my own daughter's first years," he says, squeezing me so tight in his thick, powerful arms. "On top of all else I lost, a real career, my plans… my chances with you," he says.

"She could really use a father," I admit with a shrug. John's never been that, not even at the beginning.

The offer though... It stunned Viktor. And for a

moment I worry he's not interested. That the idea —
as it would to so many men — would repulse him.

Instead, he pushes his lips to mine in a passionate
kiss that takes me all the way back to our first night
together. That blissful, perfectly fated moment
where I felt like the stars aligned to give me the life I
always dreamt of.

"Sorry," he says, pulling back. "I... I shouldn't
have presumed."

Barely before he could finish his sentence, my
mouth silences his, my tongue pressing in against his
with such a need. I don't know what it is. Maybe it's
just the intensity of the day, or the power of seeing
him again. Maybe it's still the adrenaline coursing
through my veins and making me a bit loopy.

Or maybe I'm still in love with him, even after all
these years, even after only knowing him one night.

We don't get to decide who our soulmate is, but
I'm not going to let him get away again. Suddenly
I've forgiven him of all his sins, of all the sleepless
nights I laid awake, wondering where he was, and if
he ever thought of me.

All that matters is he's back in my arms. We have
a second chance at this now.

He wraps me up in his big arms, that haven't
gotten any smaller. In fact, his forearms feel thicker,
stronger than before even. That time in prison was
spent honing himself even more than the marines
had.

Maybe it's strange to focus on the little things, like the thickness of his arms, the way the veins on his forearms bulge beneath my fingers, but I'm just soaking him all in with such relish. Ours was a love meant to happen, but which was interrupted cruelly. And I can't even blame him. He helped out Julie big time, maybe even saved her.

If only more men were willing to put it all on the line to stand up for women like her — like me — things would be so much better.

So I just savor every moment of this kiss, every little sensation of our lips smacking together. Every touch of my fingertips. The press of our bodies together.

My fingers run up his arms, to his jaw, stroking him gently as if I'm just trying to figure out if he's really here. If this is actually happening, or just another one of my many dreams, staring at him. My Prince Charming.

"I've missed you so bad," I admit, surprising even myself. "When you never showed, I thought I scared you off. That the condom breaking..."

His grasp on me tightens, those powerful arms embracing me so warmly as his smoldering eyes gaze into mine.

"Fuck no," he says crassly, to the point. "I was never happier about a moment in my life. And with the condom breaking... shit, I was eager to see it through, whatever happened. I just... I acted without thinking of the consequences. Without realizing it might cost me a possible future with you. Damn Alice, you never left my mind in prison."

He presses his lips to mine again in a sudden, passionate kiss renewed for another sweet moment.

I can feel all this relief, all this regret swirling within me. Anger that we've been so unfairly separated, that chance would put him on this horrible path. He never should've been put in such a heinous situation, especially not for just trying to stand up for someone else. That shithead rapist should've been the one serving time.

Not my sweet Viktor. Not this man with a beautiful heart, with the most gorgeous husky voice and kindest words.

It was an injustice.

But all that paled in comparison to my gratitude to have him back. To be kissing him once more.

Those big hands of his grasp my hips and together, as if we're of a unified mind, he lifts me up and I wrap my legs around his waist. He lets his palms move from my hips to my ass, touching, squeezing me as we make out frantically.

We're in his bedroom, by sheer coincidence of needing a quiet place to chat. It's spacious, big, the bed humongous, and he carries me towards it after making out with me in his arms for so long.

The two of us tumble down upon the bed, the

thick comforter seeming to swell around me as he rests over me. My big, broad-shouldered hero.

He saved me and Cierra today. Whatever he did, he did it for me and my child.

Our child.

My hands reach down, grazing across his abs before reaching the button of his pants, my eyes meeting his the entire time.

"I never thought I'd see you again."

"I never stopped dreaming I would," he responds in that deep, husky voice of his, so deliciously masculine.

Those big hands of his move up over my body, feeling me out, rubbing my waist and chest, tugging up my shirt and helping shed me of my shirt and clothes as he kisses down my neck, across my collarbone.

And just like last time, it feels so right. Like this is meant to be.

It has to be fate. It has to be. What are the odds of the world sending our lives colliding back together like this if it wasn't fate?

I unzip his pants, my fingers delving in and touching his cock, an irrepressible moan of delight escaping my lips. He feels even better than I remember, and my body quivers with excitement as his lips continue teasing across my chest.

He reaches beneath my body, undoing my bra with such a fluid motion, freeing me from its confines as his ravenous mouth sweeps in to kiss and lick at my breasts, to ease the edges of my areolas. It doesn't feel like what we had was a one-night stand five years ago. Our bodies move together like we're husband and wife parted for far too long. That's how it feels as he hungrily devours me, suckles my nipple and teases my flesh before moving down to work open my pants and get them off of me.

I release his cock just long enough for him to free me of every last stitch of my clothing, and then I look up at him. I'm bared to him, naked and vulnerable. He's taken two lives today, but I know he did it for me. To protect me.

He didn't think twice about it, about the repercussions. He could've been sent right back to jail, and we'd never have had this moment, but he didn't care. He was just worried about keeping me safe.

He's a hero. He's always been a hero. Even though his hair isn't quite the military crew cut anymore, and there's a darkness in his eyes that wasn't there when we first met, I can still see that spark in him. That boyish charm, that strong moral code.

He's my hero, and in this moment, I'm utterly in awe of him.

My mouth goes to his once more, tenderness and passion combining as I taste him. "I love you, Viktor," I whisper against his lips, sealing it with a kiss.

He's momentarily stunned by my words, and then it tumbles from his luscious lips: "I love you too, Alice. Since the moment I met you I just felt it was meant to be," he says with such passion, excitement, his heart thudding in his chest beneath my hand as it rests on his bulging pec.

It wasn't just me that felt it. This magnetism between us. He felt it too.

We're kissing again, making out madly, passionately, when he breaks away to speak.

"I don't have a condom on me," he admits. "I wasn't… I didn't expect anything like this to happen," he admits.

"Not like it really helped last time," I reply, my tone a bit joking, though really, there's a million thoughts rushing through my brain.

But the one overpowering them all is that he loves me. He's the reason the best blessing in my life is here. And he's the only one for me, I know it. I draw in my lower lip.

"What will happen if…" I ask, my voice going a bit quiet.

"I learned five years ago I can't promise what will happen," he says to me, giving me another brief kiss, the moist smack punctuating the air. "But I can promise what I'll do. And that'll be everything in my power to protect you, our daughter and any future kids we might possibly have. That's the best I can give you, Alice," he says with such deep conviction.

"But what you're involved in," I say, reality edging back in as my fingers go to his jaw. We're so close we're sharing a breath, my body pinned beneath his, so desperate to just fuck like we did when we were younger and filled with dreams.

Back then, the future spread out before us like a fabulous feast.

Can we get that back?

"I'll leave it all behind for you. For Cierra. I'll do whatever it takes to make it legit. Just as soon as I handle this threat to you and her. On all my honor, on everything I learned in the corps, I'll stay true to that vow, for yours and Cierra's sake," he says, such steely certainty in his eyes.

I believe him. Every cell in my body tells me that he's being honest, and that he'll stay true to his words.

Neither of us knows what the future will hold, but now that I have him back in my life, I don't think I can ever turn back from this. The what-ifs with him are the only chance I have at getting the future I want back.

My hand goes to the back of his head, running through his hair as my other hand travels to his cock. My fingers wrap around his girth, and I stroke him, gently. I want to savor it; savor him.

"I've never fallen for anyone like I've fallen for you. And I never want to lose you again."

"And I've never loved anyone before you, and I'm

not sure I ever could again," he says to me back in a gravelly declaration, kissing me passionately, his hands feeling my body, lavishing in my flesh. His thumb reaching in from my inner thigh, touching upon my slit, teasing my clit. "You took ownership of my heart so very, very long ago," he professes as his cock swells in my hand, so thick, so veiny, so damn needy.

"How can one night have changed everything?" I moan, my body eagerly writhing beneath him. "Just 24 hours and everything changed. And now," I kiss his throat, down his shoulder, over his pec, just trying to convince myself he's real. "Now I have my hero back."

We're almost like two horny, grabby teens again, the both of us pawing at each other excitedly. Feeling each other out, every inch, every curve and crevice. We're so ravenous, so hungry for one another.

"Memories of our night together kept me sane each and every night in my cell," he says, his dick throbbing as he circles my clit, teasing me, raising my pleasure and desire to such a height as he rocks his own hips with growing desire to enter me.

"I wanted to look for you, to find you. But I didn't want you to think it was just child support... If you ran, I didn't want you to think..." I trail off, my mind such a haze of emotions that I can barely sort through them any longer. None of it matters.

Nothing matters but us. But our future. Our family.

"I want you," I whisper. "I want you to fuck me."

"I want you. Whatever way I can have you," he confesses to me between kisses. "I wouldn't have cared if you just came after me for child support. I just wanna be in your and Cierra's life. And I'll make it work," he pledges as his thrusting hips and my hand guides him to my pussy. "I need to fuck you," he says, just a half-moment before his thick, veiny cock splits my pussy open, stretching my labia around his hefty girth.

It's been so long, and I can't remember it ever feeling so good. So right. Like now we're not just kids playing around, but adults, people with a real connection.

My arms go around his neck, and my legs around his waist, locking him in against me as I meet his intense, emerald eyes. The same eyes Cierra inherited from him.

"Never leave me," I beg him. "I need you, like this, all the time."

He begins to thrust into me, all that powerful muscle put into hammering deep into my body, filling me up and stretching me out as he moans and kisses me. The two of us become ravenous for each other, his powerful hands squeezing and groping as his beat rocks beneath us. The expensive mattress is put to the test as his balls slap against my ass noisily.

"I don't ever want to be apart from you again," he husks deeply between the loud, deep thrusts that make me moan with pleasure.

After five years, after so much has changed, and yet our bodies still work in tandem with each other. He knows just the right way to make my eyes roll back in my head, and every time my legs pull him in that fraction of an inch deeper, he moans with such delight.

We have to be quiet, for Cierra, but that makes it even more exciting, somehow. Like we're misbehaving, sneaking around.

I kiss the hollow of his throat, and trace his collarbone with my lips.

There's a mirror on the wall, and I catch sight of us in it. I don't even recognize myself at first, because we just look so good together I can't believe it. His powerful, thrusting form filling me, working with mine. Me, spread out to accommodate him, our skin dewy and glistening from perspiration, we look far better together than either of us has any natural right to look apart.

And he bites my neck, suckles it as we make love. My breasts rippling atop my chest as they rock with his hard thrusts, his thumb pressing upon my clit, making it tingle and ignite with such fiery sensations!

"You're the most gorgeous woman in the world,

Alice," he growls out in my ear before returning to his hungry assault upon my flesh.

Ever since I first laid my eyes on him, I knew he was someone special.

Ever since we touched, I knew what we had was something special.

But there's something about him coming back into my life, after all these years, that makes everything take on a new significance and importance. We're meant to be together.

A future filled with dance classes and playdates for my daughter, always putting my own needs aside, stretches and expands. Suddenly I can see a future not just for her, but for me, too. And it's all because of him. All because of Viktor.

I whimper as electricity starts to gather in my lower belly, and my limbs begin to quake. I dig my free hand into the blankets, clutching them hard as I gasp.

"Oh God, just like that," I beg.

And he does it exactly like that. He keeps that perfect rhythm going, hitting me in just the right way as I stare up at his gorgeous body, all bulging, rippling muscle so perfectly sculpted and honed. He's a killer, but he's a killer for a good cause. He's a man made fighting machine, but he's my fighting machine.

And I adore him for it.

But right now, all that perfected muscle and

practiced ability is put towards pleasuring me and I couldn't be happier to watch him pound into me. His thick cock vanishing inside my pussy with each new thrust, my narrow little cunt clinging to his cock whenever he tugs back, eager to pull him in once more as he moans and grunts.

When I can't take it any longer, my head knocks back, and my eyelashes flutter down as that awesome pleasure crashes over me. I bite down on my lower lip — hard — just to silence the scream that's brewing in my chest.

My free hand clutches him, nails digging into his flesh as I ride out my orgasm, him hitting me just so with every single thrust.

It's such an overpowering intensity and I get so caught up in the moment I almost miss the glorious sight of his hulking, muscular body twitching and coming to life with his own impending orgasm. He groans, shudders, all those rippling muscles bulge as he comes hard. His moan loud and bellowing as his cock swells and he shoots his load deep inside of me. Each new throb of that manhood another heavy spurt of his seed, and I know it.

I know the risk intimately. We've been here before, though I didn't know it at the time.

But I know what comes next. I know the worst case scenario, because I lived it, and I wouldn't have traded Cierra for the world. I'm not afraid of the worst case anymore.

I choose to have hope. For us, for him. For our family.

My mouth crashes against his again, and our intensity is nearly bruising as we kiss and nip at one another with such need, such relief.

Like before, he holds me, squeezes me in his arms and just tenderly strokes my hair and sides. The two of us draining every last sliver of pleasure from the moment as he empties his loins into me, our lips smacking noisily as we rest upon his bed.

"I'll keep you safe," he husks between kisses. "No matter what it takes."

I don't doubt him. But at the same time, that's what has me worried. Because I know he'll truly stop at nothing.

Iwake up before Alice, slip out the door without waking my daughter, who I give a kiss on the forehead to. She's angelic as she sleeps on the sofa, curled up beneath a blanket. I've missed so much of her life, but it's like I finally found a piece that was missing. A sacred part of me that was stolen from me, for doing what was right to the wrong man.

I want to linger, to watch her sleep in that beautiful peace, but I have something I need to do first. I need to give her and her mother real peace. The type of peace that will last. I don't want her to ever have to go through a day like yesterday again.

Part of me acknowledges that this whole thing can go south and this might be the last time I ever see my daughter. My daughter.

The whole premise blows me away. Makes the

world seem so wild and crazy, when yesterday it had been so dark and depressingly predictable.

I want to be there for her, learn to braid her hair so I can make her smile. I want to make her grilled cheese and teach her about the world. About all the good parts, all the things that I desperately need to rediscover myself.

But before we can have that life, I need to make sure these thugs stop bothering Alice and her. I need to put an end to the criminal scum targeting her to get at this piece of shit John, her ex.

Short of killing them all, the best way I can think of to do that is to find John myself and deliver him to these punks. It's harsh, it's cruel, but short of going on a mass murder spree, I can't think of anything else.

They won't let him or Alice go free until they have him.

I quietly shut the door behind me and lock it. Looking around, nothing seems out of the ordinary, and that puts me at ease at least. I stayed up most of the night, watching over Alice as she slumbered and just appreciating the fact that she's still here. She's survived and thrived, and she still loves me.

She called me her hero. I have to make sure that's true.

So my first stop is the next place on my list, the place I was gonna hit up after tracking John to his girlfriend's place.

Some poking around had given me the location of a storage unit that John had paid for a while back. I track it down in the early morning, which turns out to be tougher than expected.

The little storage rental place is off the beaten path. It's a sleazy area used by criminal types, folks wanting to hide things off the record. They don't accept credit cards, it's a cash only business, and I got word through a friend of Mark's. It pays to have sleazy connections I guess.

I make my way through the maze of old, worn down storage units, gun ready in the back of my pants. I don't want to use it, but as always, I come prepared.

I arrive at the storage unit, and it's not locked, at least from the outside. But when I gently test it, careful not to make a sound, it proves my suspicions: it's barred from the other side.

That means this is now a waiting game.

John's inside, but if I make a scene or alarm him, he won't be coming out. I still have the element of surprise, at least. Unfortunately, anything could happen to me out here as I brandish a gun, including police finding me. I have to be quiet. Still. Wait for him to leave.

Time ticks by agonizingly slowly, my mind continually trying to divert to thoughts of a future with Alice and our daughter. But I have to stay focused, in the present. Ready. This is where my military training really helps. People think of combat as all action, but it's not. It's boring as fuck, and you have to stay ready at all minutes of the day. Anything could change on a dime, and so I'm never lulled into a false sense of security. My senses are always alert.

It's a tough fight to keep from grinning dumbly at the thought of a real future with a beautiful, amazing woman, and our kid, but eventually — after hours of waiting — I hear John stir inside. And then… the door starts to crack open.

I crouch and slip in under the garage-style door to get at him. Quickly, I grab him by the neck and pin him to the wall.

"You're comin' with me, John," I tell him, this man who was once probably handsome, now looking and smelling like a wreck from being on the run for so long.

"I ain't got the money, pal! Leave me alone!" he whines.

"Too late for that," I tell him. "Your running off put a good woman and her daughter in danger. They nearly died because of you. You've gotta make that good."

"Fuck! She ain't my problem man! Lemme go! If they catch me…" he says, full of self-pity and not an ounce of concern for Alice and her daughter.

That makes this a little easier to do what I need to do at least.

"C'mon. Time to pay the piper," I tell him, towing him out of the storage unit and back to my car. He struggles, but he's weak. I guess he hasn't been eating much since he's been on the run, locked in that storage cube.

That works out better for me. For my family. I've gotta handle this all quickly. Before anything more might happen to Alice.

I've got a bad feeling about this all. I hope it's just because I learned that I'm a dad, and there's now two people I care more about than my own life.

I awoke to find Viktor's home empty of Viktor. I made breakfast for Cierra, but the two of us quickly grew antsy.

"Where's Prince Charming?" groans Cierra, not for the first time. I've put on her favorite shows, got her paper to color on, but still, she can sense my nerves. I don't know where he's gone, but I can only imagine, and as the minutes turn into hours, it's just getting worse.

And Cierra hates that her routine has been broken, and she's not in a familiar place anymore. It drives her up the wall to not follow her schedule, and I guess I'm partially to blame for that. After all, working nights was the best way I could spend days with her, and I tried to make each one special.

"I don't know, sweetheart. He's probably just gone to get us some lunch."

"He's been gone forever," she says, exaggerating as she slumps back against the couch. "And I miss kitty."

"I know. We'll be home to kitty soon."

Honestly, the cat's a survivor, and will definitely be fine 'til we get back home. If it'll ever be safe to go back home. I would've taken her with us, but she took off out an open window when those thugs broke in and I wasn't able to find her before we had to leave.

"Is he my daddy?"

The question shakes me from my thoughts, and I look at her seriously. My kid is intuitive, if nothing else, and I lightly stroke her curly hair.

"Maybe, honey. Maybe one day. We need to figure some things out first."

She nods at that and relaxes back for a second, lost in her own four-year-old thoughts. Unfortunately, that leaves me to my thoughts as well. I pull out my Kindle from my purse, but as I flick through the dozens of romance novels, I realize I'm definitely not in the right headspace for that.

Not when I don't know where Viktor is, nor what my future holds.

I toss it aside and pick up my phone, the battery approaching the danger zone, and I put in a call to the house mom at the club.

"Hey Rosie. I'm not going to be able to make it in tonight."

"Oh no, sweetie! Are you not feeling well? You haven't missed a day in years... and that's quite a feat in this business."

I laugh. As if I had the option of taking time off work at the best of times. The only time I can even remember was when Cierra was a baby and she had a fever of 103, and I spent the night in hospital with her. Then I had to work even harder to get out of that debt.

Strippers don't have great health insurance.

"Yea, I should be fine for tomorrow but I'll let you know."

"Okay," she says thoughtfully. "Chicken soup. It's good for the soul, you know," she says and I can't help but smile. She really is like a mother to us.

"Sure, Rosie. I'll have that for lunch."

"Good. Good. Rest up!"

As soon as the call is over, though, my mind is once more free to wander back to the growing dread in my stomach. I glance at the clock and it's already afternoon.

"What do you say we have some soup, huh?" I ask, knowing that any bachelor worth his salt had at least better have some canned soup in the cupboards. Honestly, I just crave the distraction.

But when I look in the cupboards, and then the fridge, I realize he must be living completely off of takeout, and I sigh.

"We can order in," I suggest, but Cierra shakes her head.

"No! Soup, mommy. You made us soup last week, in the fridge."

And that much is true, but the thought of going back there...

"C'mon, we'll be back soon, and we can get kitty!"

"I don't know, Cierra. What if we miss him?"

"Note," she says, handing me the pad of paper she'd been drawing on. On the front page was three stick figures, done in blue, pink and red.

"Who's this, huh?"

"You, me, daddy!"

I swear to God, Viktor, you better not disappoint this girl, I pray, and I pet her head. Maybe it would be good to head back home. I might feel a little less on edge, at least, back in my own kitchen. And if the cops were called... well, it'd just make things worse if I disappeared for a long time after two murders took place in my home. It's better to face the music now.

"Alright, honey. I'm going to leave him a note saying we've gone home."

She smiles at me, but she's a bright kid. She can hear the hesitation in my voice. Honestly, I just don't know how I'm going to handle the questions. Handle... what happened. We were innocent, it was self-defense, but innocent people don't run.

So it's time to not run.

I pack up our few belongings and we head outside to wait for our Uber.

Cierra's well-behaved as usual on the drive back, and I'm relieved when we get there to see nothing seems to be particularly out of place. There's no police presence… nothing.

We head on up the stairs into the building and the ease of it all begins to bother me.

Didn't we hear sirens the other day? Weren't they coming here?

There's no way to know that, I tell myself. But then… that might mean I'm about to open the door to a ghastly sight for Cierra.

"Just wait here, sweetie. Mommy's gotta run in and get something real quick," I tell Cierra, giving her a kiss on the forehead.

I get my key ready and prepare to head inside, taking a deep breath before I slip it in and open the door.

But instead of a grisly murder scene I'm greeted by… nothing. It's as if there were no killings on the floor. No sign of men dying. And I can't wrap my head around it at all.

I'm confused for a moment, but quickly search around, checking the rooms of my apartment. Again and again, each room is empty, no signs of blood or death. Nothing.

It sends a chill down my spine, almost as bad as if

I'd come back to the stinking corpses of the dead men.

"You almost done mommy?" Cierra says to me, standing there in the doorway, disobeying my orders to stay outside.

"Yes sweetie, just wait outside, mommy will be right there," I tell her again before shaking off my discomfort and just getting down to work. I need to grab her a few things. Some food and toys, the things I didn't bother grabbing when I was in a rush.

And luckily kitty is back, and I put her in her carrier.

Part of me wants to stick around and go back into the comfort of our home, but I know what happened here. And though I can't see the bodies or the blood, I can feel it like a ghost that's lingering over my shoulder as I gather Cierra and I's things.

I use an old duffel bag, same one I used to come here originally for a brief trip. That brief trip where I met Viktor and conceived Cierra. I stuff as much as I can fit into it before getting ready to leave.

"Oh shoot," I hiss before going to the fridge and pulling out the container of soup. This will definitely make Viktor's place a bit more like home for us both.

"Alright sweetie, mommy's ready now," I say and turn around.

"Good, we'll head right out then," the strange man says, holding Cierra in front of him. There's a gun in his free hand, out of her sight. "I expect that won't be a problem for mommy, will it?" he says with a condescending smirk.

This time I have no choice. It's not my life on the line. It's Cierra's.

I've got John in the car seat beside me; I zip-tied his wrists together so he'd be less of a problem. Nothing stopped his pleading, his pathetic begging. I'd feel bad for him except he shows no remorse for putting Alice and Cierra in danger. No concern for anyone but himself, despite landing himself in this situation.

"No no no! No man!" he cries out in objection as I pull up to the storefront that masks the headquarters for the Asian mobsters that have been tearing up Vegas in search of him. "Not these guys! Anyone but them!"

I ignore him. I don't want to give them anything, not after what they did to Alice, but I have no choice. If I want my girls to be safe, I'm going to have to give them something in return for the two men I killed.

Immediately once I'm out of the car I can see two

guys that are trying their best to look as if they're hanging around outside the shop casually stiffen. They know I'm not here for the shops supposed purpose of imported rugs and incense.

I haul John out, grasping his arm tightly as he cringes and struggles weakly.

"I'm here to see your boss," I tell them. They're both trying to look tough but they're not doing a good enough job to intimidate anyone but John. "I've got a present for him."

One of them heads on in, presumably to speak with the boss, while the other escorts me inside, taking me into a back room. But he stops me before I go any further.

"We'll wait," he says, hand still lingering near his back where he undoubtedly hides a gun. It's a waste of time really; at this distance, if it came to a fight, I'd snap his neck before he could get that thing pointed at me.

But I'm playing nice. And I'm waiting with the now dumbstruck and silent John.

Time stretches on until another thug I've not seen before comes out.

"Why should the boss see you? He's doing some important shit right now," he says bluntly.

"Tell him Mark sent me. Macario. I've got a package he's been missing, and I want to deliver it," I tell him. My buddies name seems to do the trick and the thug heads back inside.

The other man is staring hard at me, trying to make me cower, but it won't work. I might not walk out of here, but I'm doing the only thing I can to save the only people I care about, so it's worth it. I would trade my life for Alice's without a second thought.

Moments tick by slowly, and John starts to fidget again, breaking down once more, though he knows well enough to hide it a bit better this time. He knows any ounce of weakness he shows in front of these guys will be later used against him. I can't bring myself to pity him, but I wouldn't want to be in his position.

Finally, when it seems like we've been waiting for hours, the man returns and ushers us on in.

We head down a hall until we come to a door, where a big bruiser of a guy pats me down and confiscates my gun.

"You'll get it back after," he tells me.

I don't say anything. I know it's time to just play it cool and quiet. The faster this is over with, the faster I can get back to my place. I know Alice must be worried about where I've gone, but I didn't want to screw things up between us again. I just want to make this exchange and then be done with it. I wanted to be able to tell her she's safe.

I'll figure out what to do after this is all over. I'll find some way to make a straight living, something that'll give Alice and Cierra a decent life. A happy life.

I try not to smile at the idea of us all being a family as I head on inside with John in tow, finding myself in a very packed, unfriendly looking office. Behind the oversized desk made of marble sits a big guy in a black suit with two guards at his sides. Apparently these guys like working in twos.

"Well, I certainly did not expect Macario to hand over a present like this. I figured we were in competition here," he says from behind his shaded glasses, a grin on his face. It looks poisonous, even if he is playing at being pleasant.

I can't wait to get out of this life.

"This is me paying my respects," I lie. "I'll see to it that Mark's happy. I just want everyone happy."

With that, I push John towards one of the thugs, and he takes the deadbeat off my hands. He's not my problem anymore.

"So that's that then?" the mobster behind the desk asks me, not used to any generosity in our line of business.

"That's that," I say firmly. "Hopefully that eases any tension between our two organizations," I say. I might as well make it seem as if that's the reason for my 'gift'.

Silence reigns over the room for a while before he nods to his thugs and the tension eases. Just a bit. The air is still thick enough to cut with a knife, though, and I'm careful not to betray any emotions, any thoughts. I'd be foolish to underestimate the power in this room.

"Then thank you. And perhaps I'll even forgive the little shootout at one of our stores I hear Macario's operation might be behind," he says, and though it was not only Macario's operation behind it, it was me who did the shooting, I remain unfazed. I can't let a flicker of anything show or he has me.

All the same, he studies me a while before waving me off. I don't sigh in relief, but I feel it, deep in my gut. This is finally over.

"Run along then, give Macario my thanks," he says, looking to John with a sadistic smile.

I turn and head out without waiting another moment. I don't want to know what they plan to do with the jerk, but even he probably doesn't deserve it. I can't let myself feel pity, though. He was more than willing to put Alice and Cierra's life in danger just to save his own skin.

I step out of the room but behind me I hear words that make my blood boil.

"Nice of you to finally join us John," says the boss, "and here I was thinking I'd have to torture your whereabouts out of that pretty woman of yours out back."

Alice!

The door shuts behind me and without thinking, I act.

My fist is in the one guard's throat, doubling him over in pain as he struggles to breathe with a caved in larynx. The other guard has time to slug me, at least knowing better than to try and grab for his gun.

It's a brutal punch from a big guy, but I take it and roll with it. Instead of crumpling I quickly rebound and kick him in the side then grab the back of his head. I slam his face down onto my knee, breaking his nose and maybe killing him. I can't stop to check. There's no time for anything but getting back into the office. Prepared.

I grab my gun from the first guy I took down and then crack him over the back of the head with it.

I open the door to the office once more, but already, it's emptied. They've gone through the back exit, and I quickly follow through, coming to the shadowy den of the gang's operations.

It's a big open room with curtains separating the walkway I'm on from the warehouse floor below. Down below, I see the mob boss, John, several goons and most importantly: Alice. The beautiful woman of my dreams, helplessly tied to a chair.

"The woman comes with me!" I shout out, and that startles the other gangsters who look up at me. That door to the office must've had soundproofing, because they have no idea I very noisily already took down two of their own.

Even more importantly, they have no idea the

hellfire that's going to rain down upon them if they don't give me my woman back.

There's three of them, and they have the advantage of knowing this place better than I do. But I still have years of experience. Military, and prison. Combined, that experience makes me more lethal than even they know.

"He shouldn't be back here! Fire!" shouts the boss, and all hope of a peaceful mediation are gone. But then, I never really expected that was going to be how this went down.

The goons go for their guns, but I'm quicker. I blow one guy's head off before either can even open fire. John panics and tries to run, and the second goon runs after him, grabbing his shoulder and yanking him back to the ground.

The distraction, though, gives me the second I need, and I end that man's life as well.

Which leaves the boss between Alice and me.

He grabs her shoulder, tugging her in her chair and making the wood scream against the floor. She cries out around her gag, and I shoot him in the shoulder, which sends him sprawling back, losing his grip on her.

We might actually make it out of this alive, I tell myself.

But the thought comes a moment too soon, because I fail to see the goons coming into the office I just left, and there's no time to take them out first.

For the second time in as many days, I witness horrific violence like I've never known in all my life. The loud boom of Viktor's gun echoes around me as I see the first man's head erupt into a mist of blood. I shut my eyes after that to avoid seeing John shot by one of the thugs, my mouth gagged and muffling my screams of terror.

I don't see the slimy guy behind me but I hear him hit the ground after another shot from Viktor.

My hero stands up on the walkway above, and though my heart is beating like crazy I manage to convince myself for a moment that everything will be alright.

It doesn't last.

A shot rings out and Viktor hits the floor, sprawling back. I can't see if he's okay. His legs are over the walkway above, but his torso is sprawled face down through the door into the next room. More shots ring out but I feel my hair yanked back.

The chair I'm tied to topples back with a loud crash and I nearly bash my skull on the cement flooring. But the pain doesn't stop there. I watch as the angry boss clutches his bleeding shoulder with one hand and yanks on my hair with the other.

He yells at me in some foreign language I don't understand before pulling a knife from inside his coat, the steel glinting in the light. And I give up. For just a second I surrender to despair.

Until I remember Cierra. She's being held in a closet just nearby, and if I die, there's no knowing what will become of her. So dying is not an option.

I roll away before he stabs at me with the knife, and while I'm no fighter like Viktor, I've got enough strength and limberness in my legs to sprint to my feet in no time. I'm still tied to the chair, but I use it like a weapon and a shield.

I turn my back on the mobster and use it like a buffer between his knife and me, but I know that's not enough. No, I don't know it, I feel it. Everything that's happening now is instinct, and I lunged at him — backward — using the chair as a weapon.

Slamming into the guy with the chair legs, I crash him into some old metal bin behind him, but I don't relent. I keep pushing against him, one of the chair legs jabbing close to his wounded shoulder, making him cry out in pain.

He starts to recoup, but I pull away just enough to slam back into him again and make him cry out once more.

"You won't hurt my daughter!" I scream at him through my gag, but it comes out as muffled cries as I lose control of myself in all of this. I try to assault him with the chair again but be bats me away this time and I nearly lose my balance.

This wooden bulk tied to my wrists is proving a big pain, and this time I crash it against the cement floor, breaking the chair, then smash it against the wall again to bash it apart. I find strength I never knew I had as I think about protecting Cierra.

Two planks of wood are still strapped to my forearms as the mob boss struggles for his knife on the floor, but I assault him, beating him with the two wooden stakes I have as makeshift weapons.

He might be the boss of some big criminal syndicate, but he's just a piece of shit to me, and right now I'm making him pay for taking me and my girl. I don't intend to stop until he's of no danger to Cierra and me again. I'll do this for her. Because I have to.

My fury blinds me to the sound of the thud behind me though, and only when I hear the tell-tale sound of a gun cocking do I freeze up and stop.

Can a mother's rage withstand bullets? I ask myself.

The answer doesn't matter, because I'll try anyhow.

*T*hank God for the marines, because training has me hit the floor before any of these thugs can fire off a shot at me. I do the barbed-wire-crawl from basic and take cover behind the big outlandish desk the mob boss used, letting it shield me from any shots.

I stay low at first, letting them waste bullets as I formulate a plan.

There's a letter opener sticking out of a desk drawer and I take it up in hand. But one of the thugs is coming around the side of the desk, I can tell by the sliver of shadow between the floor and the base of the marble desk.

Picking up the bosses leather chair, I hurl it over the top of the desk and it distracts them. It buys me the time I need to dart around the corner and stab the letter opener into the man's inner thigh, making him cry out and fall back as blood gushes out.

His buddy is so frantic that he foolishly shoots his injured friend as he falls back, and I spring up to put two bullets into him: One in the center of his chest, the other into his eye.

But it doesn't end there.

There's another man that rushes in immediately and I put him down too, advancing on the entrance to the office as I fire. I'm running out of bullets, and every single one counts now. Any wasted bullet might be the one I need to put down the kingpin of this operation.

I need to shut that door and bar it so that no one else can get through, but once I reach it, another thug is in my face. We're too close for guns, and I head-butt him, breaking his nose and knocking him back into the guy behind him.

I fire three shots in quick succession, putting both of them down. But more will be barging in before long so I slam the door and lock it. I grab the thug's gun that fell to the floor when he died, and check for rounds. It's still full.

I can't put my trust in that lock, so I get behind the desk and put all my strength into moving it towards the front entrance. It has to be eight hundred pounds, but I push and grunt, feeling my muscles strain as I shove it slowly towards the door, barring it off.

There's no more time to spare. I can hear sounds of a struggle, and I rush back out into the warehouse area to rescue Alice… only to find she doesn't need my rescuing at all.

I spring over the railing and land down below, cocking my gun as I check the area. Alice startles and turns, ready to fight me too. She's tenacious, standing bloodied over the body of the man I just made the trade with.

"Whoa! It's me," I tell her, hands up until she calms down and I check the place out. There's three corpses, the boss brutally done in by what looks to be the remains of Alice's chair. I swell with pride at her ingenuity, but I don't let it get me fat headed. I have to make sure this room is secure.

John is suspiciously absent, a trail of blood leading the way towards a side exit. He must've made his escape during the firefight.

"We need to get out of here. Where's Cierra?" I ask.

"In there!" Alice says, pointing manically to a barred metal door in the warehouse.

I rush over, not wanting to waste a moment in saving my daughter. I remove the heavy crate blocking the door, then try the knob. It's locked but I kick it open as we shout for Cierra to step back.

It takes a few tries, but I bash open the door, breaking the lock as we shed light on the barren little room that was once a janitorial closet. Cierra is crouched in the corner, afraid, but I rush in and grab her up, handing her over to Alice.

"Mommy's here, little one," she says, her voice so soft yet filled with emotion. She looks like she's just stepped through hell, and come out the other side. I wish I could take the time to join in on their embrace, but there's no telling how many other mobsters are going to be after us.

Alice clutches Cierra against her chest, doing her best to shield her eyes from the bloody carnage all around us. Now that the immediate danger has passed, though, Alice looks to me for what to do next. I can see how lost and out of her element she is in all this, and the terror that burns in her eyes.

"Follow me," I say, wasting no time. I don't want to give them a moment to doubt. Nor a second to break down that barrier I'd put up against the door.

Alice covers Cierra's eyes as we push through the mess of the warehouse. I go to the back door, where John had made his getaway. He'd bashed open a door and ran out into the sunlight of day, which was lucky for us. It saved us precious moments on our escape.

I make sure to check the area before we scurry outside. We arrive just in time to watch John pull out of the parking lot, not stopping to save any of us. That man is no hero, but at least he will likely be spared a gruesome murder.

Leading the way around the side of the building,

I check around the corner. There, one of the thugs stands watch, and I waste no time: I put him down like a dog. Moral qualms be damned; my girl and daughter were on the line. Any man who poses a threat to us will meet the same fate.

The three of us rush ahead to my car, which is right where I left it. The only difference is that the doors are left open, probably from the gangsters searching it. But that just makes it easier for us as we pile on in, me keeping a watch over my two girls.

They both take the back, and Alice is already telling Cierra to keep low. She's a smart woman, and she clutches Cierra as she buckles them in. Alice catches my eyes in the rear view mirror, and nods. She's ready to get out of this, and so am I.

Some of the thugs are already rushing out to stop us, and I pull us out into the road, horns honking as I try to make a fast getaway. They rush for their cars, and I steer my vehicle through the lanes of traffic to put as much distance between us all as I can.

I switch my sights from the road ahead to the rear view mirror. I see the gangsters trying to weave through traffic behind us to catch up, their glitzy, expensive cars glinting in the hot Vegas sun.

Cierra squeals, but Alice comforts her as I run a red light and take us through some more of the thick traffic. I don't want us to get stuck out here when traffic gets bad. It would inevitably lead to a shootout in the middle of the day. So many witnesses, so many potential fatalities. I can't let that happen.

So we careen between cars, and all my training from overseas is put to use as I take us through the dangerous streets. Horns honk around us as I check back behind us, the thugs fall further and further behind. They can't catch up. One of them even crashes his car, his vehicle flipping as traffic comes to a crazy halt behind us.

I cringe to think of the innocent, uninvolved people that might be hurt, but that's on the thugs chasing us. Their leader is dead, their gang is over, and their persistence will accomplish nothing. There will be no reward.

Even if they killed me and my two girls, it's over for them.

Mark and his crew will sweep in and claim their territory regardless of whether I survive this mission. It's a done deal.

And that's something I'm going to have to live with. But these dominos all started falling before I realized what I actually had to lose, and now that this is done, I have to make sure I'm out. Really out.

I need to be there to see my little girl's every momentous occasion. I need to see her go to her first day of school. I need to be at every one of her performances, big and small. I need to be there for her in the night when she's sick, and when she's graduating high school...

I'm not going to miss out on those moments, and that's what guides me through the streets and away from the chaos behind us.

They've fallen behind enough that I can feel comfortable obeying the traffic laws. I can't risk catching the attention of the cops right now. Not with a hot weapon and Alice covered in blood in the backseat. I can't go back to prison, especially not for taking down those thugs who were up to so much worse than I could ever dream of.

No, all I ever dreamed of was a life with a family who loved me. And now that I have that shot, I'm not going to let them go.

My mind is already wandering to the life I dream of, the life I always wanted to settle into when I finished my tours in the marines. But distraction is the last thing I need now, cruising through heavy traffic… as the sirens of a police car resound.

ALICE

"It's the cops," I gasp, my hand going to Viktor's shoulder. His brows are furrowed, his expression serious, and he nods to me. I hug our daughter in the backseat of the vehicle as Viktor expertly maneuvers through the traffic.

We can't get caught. I'm covered in blood, and Cierra is barely able to hold on. Our lives are in the hands of Viktor. My disappeared Prince Charming, back to rescue us from things we didn't even realize we needed rescuing from.

The sirens dim in the distance. They weren't after us. In Las Vegas there wasn't much of a shortage of emergencies for the cops to handle. One man going a little too fast wouldn't even stand out to them. I breathe a sigh of relief, and relax back in the backseat of the car.

"Are we okay mommy?" Cierra asks, and it

breaks my heart how hopeful she sounds. It has been such a rough couple of days for her. And for me. For all of us.

I nod my head, stroking her hair affectionately.

"Yes, baby girl," I say as I kiss the crown of her head. "Daddy has saved us."

"Is she asleep?" I ask, looking up at Viktor expectantly. I had taken the time to grab a shower while Viktor read Cierra a story on my Kindle. I couldn't stand feeling the scuz of those criminals on my flesh.

And honestly, I just needed some alone time to cope with everything that's happened. For over four years I've been a single mom, and having someone to help...

No, not just someone. Having Viktor to help. Her father, the only man I'd ever trusted and loved. Having him to help was something special. And I was afraid that now things were settling down, maybe he'd swoop out of my life again.

Or be taken from it.

He touches my cheek, bringing me back to the present.

"Our angel is asleep," he says, putting the emphasis on our. His touch is so gentle as he strokes my jawline. "Are you okay?"

I nod, my lips curving into a smile.

"Better than okay, now that you've saved us. Do you think that's the last of them?"

"Yea," he says, his voice a bit gruff. "That's the end of it. I'll talk to my friend and make sure, and until then, we'll just stay here. A few days max."

"Small space," I say and I glance around with a smirk. The hotel we're at is small but clean, and has a separate bedroom with a queen sized bed for the three of us.

"It's not the smallest space I've been in," he says, and I can see a bit of sadness lurking in his eyes.

"You're never going back the prison, Viktor. You have me and Cierra now."

"I know," he says, his thumb tenderly brushing along my skin as his gaze bores into mine. His emerald eyes are so intense, and I feel them burn through me. Everything about him is so intense. Just like when I first met him, but his passion has built into something even greater while he was away.

The intensity doesn't scare me though. It thrills me, because it's him. Because I know just how he feels, because it's in my heart as well.

I open my mouth to speak, but he silences me with a kiss. I'm taken by surprise, but eagerly melt into it as his tongue caresses mine. When he pulls back, my lips tingle, and I'm left breathless.

"I'm going straight, Alice. No matter what it takes. I got involved with things I shouldn't have when I was desperate. Things before I had you in my life. But they're also things that brought you back into my life, so I'm not going to waste time with regrets. I'm happy for every single shitty decision I've ever made that made it so that you are Cierra are here with me."

"I have some savings," I say, and it kind of takes me by surprise. That was always my secret savings. I'd never told anyone about that.

But I'd also never felt like this before.

And he shakes his head. "As a last resort, we touch your savings."

I can't help but laugh. If I'd told John about my savings, the first thing he'd spend is that.

Viktor looks at me, confused, and I just shake my heads.

"I'm sorry, I've just never met anyone like you," I say honestly, and his eyes crinkle at the corners as he smiles at me.

He presses his forehead to mine, our breath shared as he holds me so tenderly.

"There's no one in this world like you, my sensual Aphrodite. My loving Alice."

My heart thumps harder in my chest, my breath once more stolen from me, this time just from his words. He has such a power over me. His fingers stroke my cheek as his other hand goes to my bathrobe, teasing his fingers down the center of my chest until he reaches the belt around my waist.

"I never forgot your smell. That sugary sweet

smell," he says, the tip of his nose brushing along the edge of my hair. "The feel of your hair on my face, so silky soft. Your skin," he breathes out, his voice growing heavier with lust.

I squirm, excitement building in my stomach.

"Every night I'd shut my eyes and I'd be back at the stage, seeing you for the first time as you danced. It felt like I had all your attention, and I couldn't believe my luck, just getting a glance from you."

His mouth finds the hollow of my throat, kissing me before his tongue traces along my tendons for a second. I'm at a loss of words, but it doesn't matter, because he keeps going.

"I felt like such a boy back then. Even after serving in the marines. Seeing you made me feel like I was back in high school, with a bad crush. But when you opened up to me, and told me about Alice... that's when I fell madly in love with you."

"Viktor," I whimpered as his mouth trailed lower, and then there was no more words. He gathered my nipple in his mouth, suckling on it with such a reverential expression. His gaze was on mine as his tongue swirled around the stiffened peak.

I moan softly, biting down on my lower lip so I didn't wake Cierra. She's in the other room with the door closed, but I still want to keep quiet. He grins, a devilish spark in his eyes as his other hand works its way down betwixt my thighs, stoking my fires.

He's teasing me, building me up so high with his

perfect touches. He knows just how to thrill me, somehow. Like our bodies just communicate to each other without our say so.

We took so long to get back to each other. To find one another through all the shit the world threw at us. We're different now, yet I still feel like I did that first night we met. Like this is all fate. Like this is something that was always meant to be.

Maybe he's right. Maybe regretting the missing years and all the crap I had to put up with is worth appreciating, because it brought Cierra into my life. Because it brought Viktor back into *our* lives.

I always raised her alone, like she was mine. No one else was ever allowed being a father to her. I guess some part of me always knew that one day, Viktor would be back. That I would once again get to feel my body turn to molten fire at his perfect touches, at the way he knows just how to kiss me and turn me on.

"Viktor," I whimper as his body melts into mine, his tongue teasing my nipple to hardness, letting his teeth glance against the sensitive buds and making me shiver. He tastes me like I'm a delicacy, like I'm something he never wants to forget the feel of again.

His fingers play along my sides reverentially, his touch light and teasing as he traces circles and shapes across my skin. Then he kisses down, lower over my stomach, parting my robe even more to reveal my pussy to him.

He inhales the clean, fresh scent of my body, looking up at me with such desire.

"You're always my Goddess, Aphrodite," he says reverentially before he parts my legs, angling his head up as he goes between them. I'm standing on my tip toes to give him enough room, but I don't have enough time to think about how cramped he must be between my legs, because his mouth finds my clit and sparks fly before my eyes.

I've never felt oral sex like this, from this position, and even though I feel shakey and like I might buckle over, somehow my body seems even more sensitive. I can feel everything so intensely when his tongue roams over my slit, tasting my rich honey.

He moans and I try to quiet him, but it just comes out as a languid moan. All the adrenaline from evading the cops, from escaping those kidnappers, has coiled my body up tight. With every lick of his tongue, he helps unwind me... and then wind me up in an entirely new, and much more fun way.

When his fingers find my pussy lips and part them, curling them towards my g-spot, though, there's no holding back.

"Viktor," I hiss, trying to be quiet. "Viktor, ah! Ah! If you... ah!" I gasp out, him stealing my words as he sucks my clit and rubs that sensitive spot within me until no longer can I protest, no longer can I hold it back.

My knees quiver and go weak as I start to

orgasm, his body eagerly working me up to the highest peak I've ever felt before I nearly crash down upon him. I'm almost sure I hurt him with the force of my intense spasms as the orgasm washed over me again and again and again, but he never relented. Not until I was grasping the wall for support and completely out of breath did he finally relinquish his hold on me.

And even then, he wasn't done.

"Why don't we try for baby two?" he growls as he picks me up, pushing me against the wall.

I can't help but smile broadly, wrapping my arms around him as I nod eagerly.

The past just slips away, and the future spreads out before us so huge and beautiful. We've so much time to make up for, and instead of making me feel sad, it fills me with excitement and hope.

My mouth presses against his as he grabs hold of his hard cock, bringing it between my soaking thighs and thrusting it into me. He's so huge, and I'm so wet, and our bodies just fit together so perfectly.

His tongue dances with mine before his kisses move lower, down to the sensitive part of my neck that he knows makes my toes curl. I gasp and wiggle and writhe atop his cock as he keeps piercing into me hard and fast.

"I love you," I gasp into his ear, and that just drives him on harder, his muscular body honed to make me feel so good.

It isn't long before my over sensitive body leaves me reeling through another orgasm, and my pussy squeezes his cock, milking him of his come. Begging him, with my body, to knock me up. To give us a big family. To make up for all the lost time.

And when he finally does fill me, we're left panting in each other's arms, kissing each other with such reverence and appreciation.

It's been a long journey, but we're finally home.

Just the three of us.

Several Months Later

The blindfold is snug around my eyes, the silky material blocking out all of the world. I can't see anything, and it makes my other senses more acute. Though that does little to help me. It's completely quiet, and I'm more aware of my clothing, the black dress hugging my curves.

"Are you ready?" Viktor asks before taking my blindfold away from my eyes and unveiling the sight of three towers overlooking us.

"I should've know," I tease him, leaning over the middle of the car to kiss his mouth. "You really are splurging for our anniversary."

"Wait until you see the suite. I went Penthouse this time. All the way at the top."

I laugh as I look back at the hotel he'd booked for

our special night out.

"This must've cost—"

He cuts me off, his finger on my mouth. "Don't worry about the cost. I already missed five potential anniversaries. I want to make the sixth something to always remember."

The valet arrives and takes the keys from Viktor, and he swiftly checks us into our private penthouse room.

While we wait through the process, I can't help but think of our daughter. I have to admit, it's weird being without Cierra. She's actually spending the weekend with Viktor's mom, as funny as that is. She flew in to see her son, and they had a lot of catching up to do, obviously.

It's strange, because I never expected to be able to trust Cierra with anyone else. For all her life, it felt like it was just us against the world. But now I'm finding more support, and hell, Cierra's grandma dotes on her like mad. She wasn't even a little upset to find out about her granddaughter the way she did.

Viktor and I make our way to the elevators and he hits the top floor. I squirm in my little black dress, gnawing on my lip a little. This is the elevator ride that changed my life, once upon a time. It feels like an eternity has passed, and since Viktor's return into my life, well... we've made up for a lot of lost time.

It feels like it takes forever just to get half way up

the building, and though I'm trying to be patient, he can't hold back any longer. His lips crash against mine, his fingers finding the apex of my thighs. The odds of anyone getting into the elevator going up are slim, but the risk of being caught is exciting. Especially since there are cameras literally everywhere.

Being a stripper always tickled my exhibitionist streak, but now that Viktor's with me, well... Life has changed a lot, and I've quit the club. I only have a few more months before Cierra is in school full time, and both of us want me to be able to get as much time with her as possible. Besides, we can afford it.

Viktor gave up working with his friend in crime, but for his last act of wiping out the rival gang he was given a large nest egg. Enough for us to live our dreams, to retire to a small town on the east coast and start up a business for ourselves. Viktor runs a construction company now, while I'm working on my plans to open a little seamstress and fashion store. Nobody knows our pasts; it's a fresh start.

But we came back here to Vegas to relive the memory of when we first met.

It's not easy to think about that though with Viktor's hands and lips all over me. His fingers find my clit, and he presses down on it, whispering in my ear, "I still can't believe you're not wearing panties. That thought drove me crazy all through dinner."

"That was the point," I moan back. "I was hoping

you'd take me right then and there."

He growls, his teeth finding my neck. "Careful. I just might bend you over and fuck you right here in the elevator if you keep this up."

I shiver, half wanting to beg him to but before I can utter out 'please', we arrive on the top floor and the soft ding announces us.

Still, we have to make it down the hall to the room, and that's slow going as his big, powerful hands roam over my hips and ass, his lips on my neck as I tilt my head to the side to let him kiss and suckle there, causing me to moan.

It's just a lucky thing there's nobody else roaming the hall; but then, with the penthouses so big there aren't many rooms on each floor. We make it to our door eventually, and Viktor presses me up against the wall beside it. His hard, muscular body keeps me locked there as he nips and licks my neck.

Those hands take a moment to stop and caress my belly, which has swollen from the new child on the way. It didn't take long after being reunited to see the little plus sign on the pregnancy strip. If that doesn't testify to what a virile stud I've landed, I don't know what does. Of course, there's been a lot more sex since this second pregnancy, but the deed was done by then.

"You look so beautiful when you're pregnant," he husks into my ear in a gravelly voice. "I feel so sad I missed it the first time." Slickly he manages to slide a hand over and slip the keycard into the door, unlocking it for us as he gazes into my eyes with such a fierce intensity.

"Yea, I'm going to require you not be a superhero and stand up for women in distress until this little guy's born," I say with a crooked grin. I bring my hand to his jawline, caressing it as he urges me in through the door to our elaborate suite. A bottle of champagne is already waiting for us on the table, but that's quickly getting ignored as he further backs me into the bedroom.

My backward motions aren't quick enough for Viktor though, and he just casually scoops me up into his arms, carrying me into the bedroom. Years in the marines, more in prison and now months working in construction have sculpted him into a perfect mountain of hard, stony muscle, and even with my pregnant belly, I'm like a doll to his bulging biceps.

He lays me onto the bed, kissing my lips still as he slowly pulls back to begin undoing his tie and stripping away his jacket and shirt. He unveils all those rippling, bulging muscles for my eyes to soak in. It really helps me appreciate what it's like on the other side of an erotic dance, because even though he's certainly not giving me a lap dance, it's just so exciting to see him peel away the clothes to unveil the gorgeous muscles beneath.

I'm transfixed, my mouth hanging open as I

watch. Oh, sure, we fuck all the time at home in between Cierra's naps and late at night. But this is vacation sex. Vacation without a youngster sex. I finally get to appreciate Viktor's beautiful body, and how badly I want him.

Those large hands of his move on down to unbuckle his belt and my eyes trail along that little sprinkling of hair, that treasure trail that leads me to the parting of his pants to see the thick bulge and snaking shaft beneath the cotton of his boxer-briefs.

He's still the biggest man I've ever seen, and I reach out to press my hand atop his thick cock, to feel the pulse of heat, the throb of his arousal before I curl my fingers into the waistband and tug it down. That meaty dick springs out before me as he reaches to tug my dress down from my shoulders.

"So much has happened since we were last here," I murmur as his mouth lands upon my shoulder. He teases me, trailing kisses along the cusp of my breasts. "We were such different people back then."

His eyes meet mine and I can see a wicked grin forming on his face. "And now I have you right back here where I want you. Just in time for our second date."

I laugh, but when his teeth find my erect nipple and he tugs it, he takes my breath away.

"Two pregnancies and six years later, I finally get the date you stood me up for," I grin, and he suckles my areola in response.

"Hey," he growls, pressing me back onto the bed as he hikes up my dress and gets over top of me, pinning me back. "The Las Vegas police stood you up. I'd never let my lady down if I could help it," he says, brandishing that thick cock as he squeezes one of my heavy, swollen breasts, flicking a nipple and making me gasp.

"Yes, sir," I say teasingly as my fingers wrap 'round his cock, my gaze glued on his. "I think what matters most is making up for all those lost days and nights. So, soldier... what are you into?"

"You," he husks gruffly, his dick swelling in my hand as he leans down and flicks his tongue over my other nipple, then suckles it briefly. "Or at least I will be in just a moment..." he grins at me deviously, his powerful body over me as he lowers himself down, that thick, bulging purple crown atop his manhood aiming for my womanhood. "You've got no idea what your tight little pussy does to me."

I bring my hand down to my pussy, drawing the wetness out before I bring my fingers to his lips. "I'm guessing we have similar effects on each other," I tease as he suckles my flavor off of me with a loud, low moan of approval. My taste makes his cock pulse wildly with excitement.

"I love you," he says at last as his lips smack off of my fingers, his dick descending down, the tip kissing my slit before he sinks himself into me. That massive shaft of his, even after screwing like bunnies each day for months now, even after bearing his child once already, still so thick. It stretches my tight canal, makes me moan as he gives a husky moan of pleasure himself atop me.

"I love you, Viktor," I say as my arms wrap around his neck. "My prince charming." My lips go to his shoulders and I bite down to silence my moan before I remember... I'm not at home anymore. I can scream out his name at the top of my lungs, and I do once he rocks back those hips of his, tugging my labia with him only to thrust in again.

He's huge, in every way, and though he's being gentle with me because of my advancing pregnancy, he doesn't have to be rough to make me squeal, moan and scream. He's too much of a beast in the flesh to need to be harsh. Just that rising pace of his pounding into me, that steady slap of his groin and balls to my flesh, it's enough to make me feel like the pleasure is being ripped out of my nerve endings and into my brain.

And the sight of all that hard muscle and sinew rippling, bulging, it's a better sight than anything you could pay for.

I don't hold back this time, the air filled with my screams and moans of pleasure. My fingernails carve half-moons into his back as I grip him tight. Every thrust sends electricity through my body, my pussy wrapped tightly around him. It reminds me of the first time, all of the passion just exploding between us, but it's matured and turned into something new. Something exciting and arousing all on its own.

Viktor takes hold of my thighs, lifting my legs and spreading them open and back so that he can really slide right in deep without any hindrances. It lets him pound into me exactly as he wants to, burying his thick cock in me nearly to the hilt but holding back just that tiny bit to keep from battering my pregnant womb.

He's a powerful man, but he's a man in control. Even as I see the tension in his muscles, the conflict on his face to want to let loose and rut me wildly.

"I'm so damn glad that condom broke," he growls at me deeply. "I want to keep you knocked up for the rest of your life if that's what it takes to keep you as mine."

I love it when he's crass and he knows it. It brings another moan to my lips, another pulse of my pussy as my heart begins to race. A one night stand. That's all we were supposed to be. But fate had other plans. It knew we were soulmates from that very first second I laid eyes on him so long ago.

"I never want to be without you a single day," I purr seductively into his ear as my fingers go to the root of his cock. He can't fit it all inside me, and I wrap a couple fingers and my thumb around the base, giving him a squeeze.

That added grip makes him groan out louder, arching his neck back. And I can feel by the swell in his shaft that he's getting closer, his balls tightening as he reaches towards that climax.

"You didn't have to knock me up to keep me. I've been yours ever since our first time."

He slides his own thumb in towards my clit in response, pressing upon that sensitive bud and driving me towards my own orgasm as he plows into me. Harder, faster, a little more erratic as he moans and twitches with excitement.

"Take it," he growls, and at last he tumbles over that precipice, burying his cock in me as much as he can as he unloads a thick, creamy blast of his seed, then another, and another. Each one I can feel in my fingers as I grasp him, stretching out my digits as he swells.

And our fingers mingle to bring me over that edge shortly after. Orgasms since I got pregnant have been so much more intense, my entire body so sensitive to all stimuli. I scream and wail as his fingers and mine keep those jolts of pleasure shocking through me over and over.

We're a panting, quivering, glistening mess on the penthouse bed by the time we're done, but Viktor is showering me with tender kisses and adoring touches, caressing my cheek and hair, stroking my pregnant belly.

"I love you Alice," he says again in such a deep, sincere voice. "I want to spend the rest of my life with you and the life beyond, if one awaits me," he says, reaching over into his blazer strewn at the foot of the bed.

And then my heart skips a beat as I watch him take out a tiny, black velvet box.

"Please Alice," he says, opening it up and showing me the most lavish diamond ring I've ever seen in person, twinkling in the dim light of the room. "Make me complete. Be mine until the end of time, and I'll be yours forevermore."

I don't know if it's the pregnancy hormones or not, but he didn't even finish before tears were streaming down my cheeks. Here we are, naked and prone, but I've never felt more loved and protected than when I'm with him, laying in the afterglow of our lovemaking.

My hand goes to my mouth and I just start nodding, words failing me in this most perfect moment. His hand finds mine, and the ring hovers around my manicured nail while he waits.

"I'll be yours 'til the end of time," I finally sputter out, my voice cracking and filled with sobs.

He presses the ring down and his mouth finds mine, our engagement sealed with a messy, perfect, lust filled kiss.

We make love again, then again. It's too late to call back home and let Viktor's mom and Cierra know about the engagement, so we've nothing to do but express our love over and over again. And when I'm spent and can take no more, Viktor holds me, and we talk about the future as we watch the sun rise over Vegas. The fiery ball crests over the mountains to light up the desert and glint off the many tall, extraordinary buildings.

It's a few hours earlier back on the east coast where Cierra is, so we clean ourselves up and call back home for a video chat. The bright faces of Cierra and Viktor's mom smile at us.

Every little plan we had for how we'd tell them flew out the window when I just flash the giant ring on my finger and Cierra's eyes bulge. Even at her age, she knows what it means and she claps excitedly.

"You're my daddy for real now!" she says.

"That's right," Viktor remarks with a bright happy smile, his hand resting on my hip.

But his mom has a knowing look and a wry smile that leads me to believe she knew all about his proposal.

"I couldn't ask for a better daughter-in-law," she says honestly. "I'm so glad my son found and chose you, Alice. You're every mother's dream for her son."

Her words bring a tear to my eye. Never did I think leaving it all behind to become a dancer in Las Vegas would lead to such an adventure. I found true love, a beautiful child, another bun in the oven, and real, true fulfillment.

And I can't wait to settle down and just be a family.

ALSO BY ALEXIS ABBOTT

Romantic Suspense:

ALEXIS ABBOTT'S BOUND TO THE BAD BOY SERIES:

Book 1: Bound for Life

Book 2: Bound to the Mafia

Book 3: Bound in Love

ALEXIS ABBOTT'S HITMEN SERIES:

Owned by the Hitman

Sold to the Hitman

Saved by the Hitman

Captive of the Hitman

Stolen from the Hitman

Hostage of the Hitman

Taken by the Hitman

The Hitman's Masquerade (Short Story)

ROMANTIC SUSPENSE STANDALONES:

Criminal

Ruthless

Innocence For Sale: Jane

Redeeming Viktor

Sights on the SEAL

Rock Hard Bodyguard

Abducted

Vegas Boss

I Hired A Hitman

Killing For Her

The Assassin's Heart

Romance:

Falling for her Boss (Novella)

Most Wanted: Lilly (Novella)

Bound as the World Burns (SFF)

Erotic Thriller:

THE DANGEROUS MEN SERIES:

The Narrow Path

Strayed from the Path

Path to Ruin

Alexis Abbott is a Wall Street Journal & USA Today bestselling author who writes about bad boys protecting their girls! Pick up her books today if you can't resist a bad boy who is a good man, and find yourself transported with super steamy sex, gritty suspense, and lots of romance.

She lives in beautiful St. John's, NL, Canada with her amazing husband.

Want to keep up to date with Alexis Abbott's new releases, sales, and giveaways? Want a **Free** bad boy romance novel? Subscribe to Alexis' VIP Reader List: http://alexisabbott.com/newsletter

facebook.com/abbottauthor

twitter.com/abbottauthor

instagram.com/alexisabbottauthor

bookbub.com/authors/alexis-abbott

pinterest.com/badboyromance

9 781988 619231